JOE COLTON'S JOURNAL

An enormous weight has just been lifted from my tired old shoulders. I just received an anonymous message assuring me that my missing foster daughter, Emily, is alive and well and will return home soon. I've shared the news with my eldest son, Rand, and also confided my concerns about my crumbling marriage. Rand seems to know more about his mother's bizarre behavior than he's letting on, but he'll tell me what's on his mind when he's good and ready. Rand always did me proud, but I do worry about his ruthless determination to succeed. He needs a good woman to show him what's important in life— and he may have found her in his feisty new legal assistant, Lucy Lowry. Why, this pretty spitfire lights up the office with her spunk and energy, and she is no pushover, let me tell you! She has zero tolerance for Rand's overbearing ways, which of course doesn't sit well with my hot-tempered son. Mark my words, all that simmering sexual tension between them is bound to set off some major fireworks....

About the Author

VICTORIA PADE

is a native of Colorado, where she continues to live and work. Her passion—besides writing—is chocolate, which she indulges in frequently and in every form. She loves romance novels and romantic movies—the more lighthearted the better—but she likes a good, juicy mystery now and then, too. She particularly enjoyed being included in the Colton series for the opportunity to write a book with a more cosmopolitan feel to it and for the chance it gave her to research Washington, D.C.

From Boss
to Bridegroom

Victoria Pade

Published by Silhouette Books
America's Publisher of Contemporary Romance

Special thanks and acknowledgment are given
to Victoria Pade for her contribution
to THE COLTONS series.

SILHOUETTE BOOKS
300 East 42nd St.,
New York, N. Y. 10017

ISBN 0-373-38708-3

FROM BOSS TO BRIDEGROOM

Visit Silhouette at www.eHarlequin.com

Printed in U.S.A.

THE COLTONS

Meet the Coltons—
a California dynasty with a legacy of privilege and power.

Rand Colton: *The beast.* A powerful mover and shaker, this attorney is used to getting his own way—until his new assistant quickly turns his well-ordered life upside down!

Lucy Lowry: *The beauty.* Capable of giving as good as she gets, Rand's new assistant tempts him like no other woman he's ever met. And it's not long before her boss has only one item on his "to do" list—to move their relationship from the boardroom to the bedroom....

Dr. Martha Wilkes: *The baffled therapist.* Her patient calls herself Patsy Portman, and yet none of her memories match that woman's life. Is this a case of multiple personality disorder...or something more nefarious?

THE COLTONS

Theodore Colton m. 1940 Kay Barkley
1908–1954   1919–1954

Ed Barkley m. 1916 Betty Barkley
1895–1966   1899–1970

THE McGRATHS

Jack McGrath m. Maureen O'Toole
1906–1988   1935   1915–1989

- Liam, 1936–
- Collin, 1938–
- Maude, 1940–
- Francis, 1942–
- Peter m. 1970 Andie Clifton
  1949–   1951–
  - Austin, 1971–
  - Heather, 1976–

Graham Colton 1946– m. 1970 **Cynthia Turner** 1941–
- Jackson, 1973–
- Liza, 1975–

Edna Kelly m. 1945 George Portman
1920–1970   1915–

Meredith Portman 1949–

Patty 1949–

Joseph Colton 1941– m. 1969

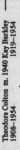

Foster Children
- Chance Reilly, 1967–
- Tripp Calhoun, 1968–
- Rebecca Powell, 1968–
- Wyatt Russell, 1969–
- Blake Fallon, 1969–
- River James, 1970–
- *Emily Blair, 1980–

Natural Children
- Rand, 1970–
- Drake, 1972–
- Michael, 1972–1980
- Sophie, 1974–
- Amber, 1976–

- Jewel, 1969–
  (by Ellis Mayfair)
- *Joe, Jr., 1991–
- *Teddy, Jr., 1993–

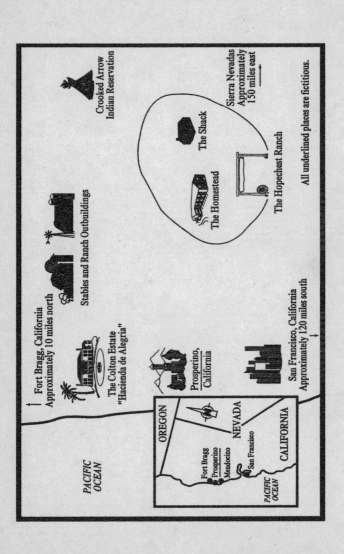

Crooked Arrow
Indian Reservation

Sierra Nevadas
Approximately
150 miles east

The Shack

Fort Bragg, California
Approximately 10 miles north

Stables and Ranch Outbuildings

The Homestead

The Hopechest Ranch

The Colton Estate
"Hacienda de Alegria"

Prosperino,
California

San Francisco, California
Approximately 120 miles south

All underlined places are fictitious.

PACIFIC
OCEAN

OREGON

NEVADA

CALIFORNIA

Fort Bragg
Prosperino
Mendocino

San Francisco

PACIFIC
OCEAN

One

"Well, of course, you know I need the money. There were all the moving expenses and the cost of the mailings and ads for the business. And there's no way of knowing how long it will be before I get any kind of work, but—"

"But nothing. The job is only until Rand finds someone else, and it'll give you the opportunity to become familiar with downtown, plus get your foot in the door with one attorney and make contacts with several others. That's what you want, isn't it? Then they'll send their research work your way and you'll have your start here."

Here was Washington, D.C.—Georgetown to be specific—and Lucy Lowry had to admit that her aunt, Sadie Meeks, was right.

Lucy had just moved cross-country from California with her four-year-old son Max and the move itself had been expensive. Now that she was settled into one of the four row houses her aunt had invested in, she needed to concentrate on earning an income, hopefully doing legal research so she could work out of her home and still be with Max as much as possible. But until all her efforts to drum up that kind of business succeeded, she intended to do secretarial work and/or bookkeeping to make ends meet. Which was exactly what her aunt was proposing—the secretarial work, anyway.

"Being downtown is the problem," she said to her aunt. "Not only would I not be working out of the house, I wouldn't even be nearby."

Sadie waved away her concern. "But it would only be for a little while. I told you I spoke with the director of the day care and they'll let you leave Max there as a favor to me for reading to the kids once a week and because the director is my old sorority sister. It's a very exclusive day care and there's a mile-long waiting list that we're circumventing. Max will get the chance to meet some friends of his own. And he can stay with me some of the time, too. We'll work on my Gameboy skills."

Sadie paused and switched gears. "Do it as a favor to me, if nothing else, darling. I'm enjoying my retirement and as fond as I am of Rand Colton, I just don't feel like going back to work. But he's in such a bind...."

Lucy knew she couldn't argue with that tack. Her

aunt—her *favorite* aunt—had only recently bought the row of four town houses and offered one to her and Max rent-free. Sadie had insisted that the rent on two of the places paid the payment on all four and if Lucy and Max moved to Georgetown to help manage the properties, particularly when Sadie traveled, it would more than make up for the lack of rent on the town house they'd occupy. Because of that arrangement Lucy could afford to freelance rather than work a nine-to-five office job and so she'd jumped at the offer. But now she couldn't very well refuse to do Sadie a favor in return.

"Just interview with Rand," Sadie urged. "Who knows, you may not even get the job. And even if you do, it's really only a matter of cleaning up the messes a string of incompetent secretaries have left behind since I retired. Rand will be looking for someone else in the meantime. It might only be a few days before a wonderful whiz of a secretary walks through the door and you'd be finished just that quick. But he says he's going crazy with the people the temp agency sends him."

"I still don't understand why he's had such bad luck with secretaries."

"I won't lie to you, he isn't an easy man to work for. He and I got on just fine but only because I took most of his bluster with a grain of salt. Deep down he has a good heart, but it's not always evident behind his brusque manner. And he's quite demanding. But then he's a man, after all, and even the best of them need some taking care of."

"It sounds more like the description of a big baby. A big *spoiled* baby," Lucy commented with a laugh.

"He's a long way from being a baby," her aunt answered with a hint of innuendo in her voice. "He's all man. All very formidable man. He carries a killing caseload and works insane hours, then can party until dawn and still make an impressive appearance in court by nine. He just doesn't seem to understand that not everyone can keep the same pace or accomplish all he can. Plus, he's blunt and outspoken. I've heard him called arrogant. And he doesn't suffer fools gladly. But I wouldn't be throwing you into the lion's den unless I knew you were up to it. Besides," Sadie added as if she were sharing a confidence, "he's one of the most handsome men you'll ever meet. So when he's at his worst just sit back, take in the scenery and tune him out."

Not an easy man to work for? Brusque manner? Demanding? Formidable? Blunt, outspoken, arrogant?

And that was coming from a woman who considered herself Rand Colton's biggest fan.

Rand Colton had to be a bear of a boss.

"Please, darling. I've given all my work clothes to charity and I've grown accustomed to lounging around in my bathrobe until midmorning. I just don't want to go back to work. But Rand really needs help right now."

Lucy narrowed her eyes at her aunt. "You don't have an ulterior motive, do you? That business about how handsome he is—that was just to soften the blow of his personality flaws, right?"

Sadie was as tall a woman as Lucy was, both of them stood a full five-foot-six-inches, but where Lucy was slender, Sadie was more plump, with round apple cheeks that puffed out even more with the smile she granted her niece.

"No ulterior motives," Sadie vowed. "I know you've sworn off men."

"I haven't 'sworn off' men," Lucy said, taking issue. "That makes me sound bitter and extremist, and I'm neither of those things. I have merely opted to—"

"Dedicate yourself for the moment to Max. I know. You've told me once or twice or fifty times. Not that I blame you for a lack of interest in men after what Max's father did. But believe me, Rand has more than enough female companionship and I'm the last person who would set up my own niece with such a playboy. This is strictly selfishness on my part. I'm trying to get him the assistance he needs without being the one to provide it myself."

Lucy stalled for another moment just for effect and then said, "All right. I guess you can arrange an interview."

"Done! Three o'clock this afternoon. I'll drive you in myself and take Max for ice cream while you meet Rand."

Lucy laughed again. "You've already arranged for the interview. Very sure of yourself, aren't you?"

"It'll work out for the best. You'll see. Now go change into a suit. You have to look professional. Rand is a stickler for that."

"Oh good, a stickler, too," Lucy said facetiously, adding stickler and playboy to the already long list of things that *didn't* recommend Rand Colton to her.

"Just keep thinking of all the other attorneys you'll encounter to hand out your card to," Sadie advised airily. "Now scoot! You don't want to be late. He can't abide anyone being late either."

"I think I should have two scoops on-account-a when you go someplace dressed like that we don't eat dinner till way late in the nighttime and by then I'll be hungry again."

Lucy craned around to look at her son, strapped into the back seat of Sadie's car by seat belts.

Max was small for his age but precocious. He seemed more like four going on forty most of the time, making it difficult to argue with his reasoning.

"It's true that I dress like this to go to work. But today I'm just going to talk to a man, so it won't take that long. We'll have dinner at the same time we do every night now."

Max wrinkled his pert little nose.

Lucy thought that even if she weren't his mother she'd think he was adorable. He had chipmunk cheeks, big blue eyes that stared out at her from behind owlish eyeglasses, and whisk-broom brown hair cut close to his head.

"Two scoops, okay?" he said as if she should grant permission despite their previous exchange.

"Sorry. One scoop, buddy."

"But what if they have the butter brickle kind *and*

the bubble-gum kind? Then I should have a scoop of each and eat supper better tomorrow.''

''If they have both kinds you can have one scoop of one kind now and we'll get the other kind to take home for tomorrow.''

Max grinned victoriously, as if that had been what he was angling for all along.

Seeing it made Lucy's heart balloon. He had a silly habit of biting the tip of his tongue between his front teeth when he grinned like that and it was so cute she couldn't believe it. He also had heartbreaker dimples in each chubby cheek that made him look irresistibly impish.

''What if there are *three* kinds?'' he suggested as if he knew her defenses were down.

''Quit while you're ahead,'' she advised as both she and Sadie laughed.

Sadie pulled to a stop at a red light and nodded to the huge chrome and glass high-rise building on the next block. ''Rand's office is in there. I'll just drop you off out front. The ice-cream parlor is two blocks farther down in the lobby of the redbrick building. They have underground parking there so I'll be able to get a spot. Why don't you walk over and meet us when you're finished?''

''You don't want to come up and say hello?''

''Rand and I had a nice chat on the phone. I know how busy he is. I don't want to bother him with a drop-in.''

When the light turned green, Sadie pulled through the intersection and eased the car to the curb in front of Rand Colton's building. "He's on the twenty-third floor, Suite 2300. Good luck."

"I probably need it," Lucy said wryly. Then, with a quick glance back at Max again, she added, "Be good for Aunt Sadie."

"He'll be fine," Sadie answered as the car behind them honked.

Lucy took that as her cue and hurried out of the vehicle so her aunt could get going again.

As she entered the imposing building, she checked her watch. She had twenty minutes to spare and while she had no intention of being late, she also didn't want to appear overeager.

So with time to spare, she found a rest room in the lobby and went in to check her appearance.

She'd worn what she considered her power suit— a navy blue formfitting jacket with a high split-collar that helped disguise the length of her neck, and straight-leg slacks to match. She knew that some schools of thought held that a woman should wear a skirt but she didn't subscribe to it. Partly because she felt more comfortable—and more confident—in pants, and partly because on her eighteenth birthday she'd taken a dare from a friend and been tattooed on the inside of her right ankle. It was a tasteful rose tattoo, barely an inch from bud to stem and not readily noticeable, but depending on how conservative the interviewer was, it could be detrimental.

She freshened her lipstick. It was a pale shade of burnished red and, along with mascara and blush, was the only makeup she wore.

She was glad to see that her blue eyes—the same shade as Max's—were clear of the slight redness an allergy had caused the day before. But she closed them for a moment to fight the burning that was a continuing result of having cleaned out the dusty attic.

Her shoulder-length mahogany hair was ordinarily a hard-to-tame mass of spiral curls, but for interviews she always wrestled it into a topknot. If she left it loose, she had a tendency toward a come-hither sort of appearance that some men read as a sexual invitation. It wasn't an impression she wanted to give.

She checked her watch again—2:50—and decided it was time to take the elevator to the twenty-third floor.

On the way up she felt the same anticipatory tension she always experienced when facing a job interview, but she fought it by reminding herself that this was only a temporary position and even if it could be an important step in making contacts in the legal profession, she already had a foot in the door in the form of her aunt.

But still, knowing in advance that Rand Colton was a difficult man put her on edge. She took several deep breaths, hoping that would help and stepped off the elevator when the doors opened.

Suite 2300 was to her right, at the end of the hallway. Two oversize oak doors unlike any others on the floor marked the entry and a simple, elegant gold nameplate announced Rand Colton, Attorney At Law.

Lucy took a last deep breath, reached for the ornate gold knob and entered the office to the distant sound

of female sobbing and male shouting. "It was a simple enough task—cancel an appointment. Instead you
let the CEO of a major company come all the way
down here when I was in court. You may just be a
temp but surely someone somewhere told you that
when your employer tells you to call a client and
cancel an appointment you should actually pick up
the phone and do it."

More sobbing surrounded a pitiful, "I forgot."

"You *forgot?*"

The booming male voice was loud enough to hurt
Lucy's ears and she wasn't even in the same room.

"You rattled off so many things in such a hurry I
couldn't write them all down fast enough and then
you left and I tried—"

"Trying isn't good enough! Do you know what
that man's time is worth?"

Apparently the temp had no answer to that because
rather than feebly defending herself any longer, she
came rushing out of the inner office, snatched her
purse from a desk drawer and ran past Lucy out of
the suite.

Definitely a bear of a boss. Assuming, of course,
that the man delivering the tirade was Rand Colton.

"Incompetence and idiocy. Where do they find
these people?"

This last part wasn't a shout, it was more a remark
to himself that Lucy could still hear as she stood in
the reception area.

If it hadn't been so close to three o'clock by then,
she would have slipped out of the office and given

the man she hadn't yet set eyes on a moment to calm down before their meeting.

Just then the man came storming out of the inner office. Without so much as a glance in Lucy's direction he charged the large oak reception desk to pound punishingly on the computer keyboard. He didn't show any indication that he'd even realized she was there, but with his eyes still on the computer monitor, he said in as derogatory a tone as she'd ever heard, "And who are you?"

Patience, she counseled herself.

"I'm Lucy Lowry, Sadie Meeks's niece. We have a three o'clock interview."

"Is it that late already?" he barked, while still assaulting the keyboard.

"I'm afraid it is."

"Well, I don't have time for you right this minute. I have to smooth some ruffled feathers. Sit down and wait."

"Excuse me?"

Lucy hadn't intended to use such an imperious tone with him. It had just come out that way in response to the increasing outrage she was feeling. But she didn't regret it. No one spoke to her like that and got away with it.

Apparently her tone wasn't lost on the man because he stopped what he was doing, stood up straighter and looked directly at her for the first time through cobalt-blue eyes that might have caused a lesser person to cower.

But Lucy merely stood her ground.

His very sharp jaw pulsed as if he'd just clenched his teeth, but he adopted a more businesslike attitude. "Please take a seat while I make a phone call, Ms. Lowry, and I'll be with you as soon as possible."

That was more like it.

"I'd be happy to," she informed him, turning on her heels to sit on one of the six overstuffed chairs that lined the walls beneath paintings she recognized as originals of high-quality artists.

When he found what he was looking for on the computer—apparently a phone number—he sat in the desk chair and picked up the phone.

Lucy had to admit as she was forced to overhear the conciliatory call, though, that he handled it with aplomb. He put minimal blame on the temp, accepted the responsibility for having heaped too many things on her at once, and he did it all without playing the sycophant, which someone else in a position of having needlessly inconvenienced an important client might have.

Lucy was impressed.

She also had the chance to take a good long look at him as he made dinner plans with the man on the other end of the line.

She'd realized how tall he was when he'd stormed into the waiting room—an intimidating six feet two inches of well-muscled, broad-shouldered self-possession. Along with his striking blue eyes and chiseled jawline, he had dark hair the color of espresso without cream, full eyebrows, an aquiline nose and intriguing lips—the upper one much thinner than the lower.

Her aunt had not been exaggerating when she'd said he was handsome. Handsome didn't begin to describe the whole package of incredible good looks, exquisitely honed physique and a presence that filled the room. Packaged in a gray Armani suit, a paler gray shirt as crisp as the moment it had come off the dry cleaner's press, and a silk tie that no doubt cost as much as Lucy's entire outfit, he was something to behold.

But only in a purely observational, objective way, Lucy was quick to assure herself. After all, it wasn't as if she were interested in the man himself. No matter how incredible-looking he was. Number one, she had put romance on hold in her life to raise her son and had no intention of changing that for anyone. And number two, even if she hadn't, she knew better than to get anywhere near a personal relationship with a man like Rand Colton.

But the scenery was most assuredly fine. Her aunt hadn't been wrong about that.

Lucy just wasn't sure if it would be fine enough to compensate for his bad behavior if she were ever on the receiving end of his tirade.

His phone call finally ended, and without a word to her, he made another for dinner reservations at a restaurant Lucy had seen on the news just the night before. It had been touted as the finest D.C. had to offer, but according to the report, people were waiting up to six months to get in. It only took the mention of his name to get him a table for four at eight.

Then he hung up for the second time, lunged out of the chair and rounded the desk to perch a hip on its corner and focus his total attention on her just that quick.

"So you're Sadie's niece. I didn't know before I talked to her yesterday that she had one."

"Lucy Lowry," she repeated, unsure if he'd remembered her name. "And since I just heard you on the phone, I know now that you're Rand Colton."

"Sorry for not introducing myself. Yes, I am."

That seemed to stall the conversation as he studied her so intently she wanted to squirm. But she didn't. She wouldn't give him that advantage.

Then he said, "Sadie tells me you've been an executive secretary and done some legal research in the past, that legal research is what you want to do exclusively now but that you might be able to spare some time to straighten things up around here and keep me going until I can find someone else."

"Sounds like my aunt did the interview for me."

"She says you're as good as she is."

"We've never worked together so I wouldn't know if that's the truth or not. But I am good."

That brought a slow-as-molasses, one-sided smile from him, as if she'd said something with a double entendre he hadn't missed and wouldn't let go.

Lucy sat up straighter, anticipating an inappropriate comment.

But he surprised her and kept his wayward

thoughts—if that was what had been behind his expression—to himself.

Unfortunately she was also aware of an unwarranted little flutter of something wholly unprofessional that that devilish quirk of a smile set off in her. And maintaining a stiff posture didn't help that one iota.

"Did Sadie warn you about what I require in the way of a secretary?"

"She said you were brusque and demanding."

He laughed, a deep, barrel-chested sound that seemed to warm the air all around them. "Honesty. I like that. Did she warn you about the amount of work I need from a secretary-slash-assistant-slash-researcher and the kind of hours I keep?"

"Basically. But you should know that I absolutely will not work past five o'clock."

That sobered him and pulled his brows nearly together over those stunning eyes of his. "Okay, I'm going to go out on a limb here because you're Sadie's niece and this is somewhat of an informal interview. I'm in a mess and the last thing I need is another single mother running through this office. I've had my fill of them in the last two months. Every time I turn around they're on the phone with one of their kids or worrying about them or leaving to do something with them. So I'm not asking if you have children. But if you do, do us both a favor and just say thanks but no thanks here and now."

Max was not something Lucy hid from anyone and it was on the tip of her tongue to admit that yes, she was a single mother. But at the same time it also occurred to her that it was none of Rand Colton's business one way or another. Being a parent—even a single parent—would not interfere with the job he wanted her to do for him. On the other hand, as vehement as he was on the subject of single mothers, Lucy thought that it could very well influence his opinion of her and that could reflect down the road in referrals or derogatory comments he might make to other attorneys she could be courting for research work.

She didn't deny having a child—that was something she would never do. But since he was leaving it up to her to give him the sign that she did have a child by turning the job down, she just didn't do it. Instead she said, "I assure you I will not let personal calls interrupt my work and you'll get very full days out of me. They'll just end at five."

"I work later than that."

"I don't."

Lucy met him eye to eye in the stare-down that followed, not so much as blinking before he did. Yes, she'd come to realize working with this man would give her just the opening and contacts she needed to garner future research work and so the job was more valuable to her than she'd originally thought, but it wasn't so vital that she would neglect Max because of it.

Rand Colton was the first to break the standoff.

"You know I'm under the gun here. The library back there—" he threw a nod over his shoulder in the direction of the corridor behind him ''—is full of files that need to be updated, sorted and put away. I don't know how people can tout themselves as competent when they don't even seem to know the alphabet. I'm working on several big cases and, as I'm sure you've gathered just since arriving, my scheduling is a mess.''

''I can take care of all that.''

''But not after five.''

''I'll give you one late night to get things under control. But after that I leave at five. No matter what.''

''Are you rushing off to a husband or a boyfriend who can't fix his own dinner?''

''Is exposure of my private life a factor in doing your filing?''

He sized her up again but his expression was still more amused than not.

''So I can take your services or leave them, but anything outside of the office is off-limits. Is that it?''

''I'm only temporary help,'' she reminded him. ''I don't see why too many details need to be explored for me to come in on that basis.''

He went on piercing her with those deep cobalt-blue eyes that seemed more remarkable the longer Lucy looked into them. But in the end he conceded.

''I'm trusting Sadie not to steer me wrong about your skills, so I guess I'll have to be satisfied with days that end at five. But you'd better be as good as your aunt says you are.''

''So I'm hired?''

"You're hired. Can you start tomorrow?"

"On a Friday?"

He nodded. "And stay tomorrow night the way you said you would."

Rand Colton, playboy, wanted to work on a Friday night?

"All right," Lucy agreed because it wasn't as if she had anything planned. "Then I'll be here at eight tomorrow morning."

"Sadie didn't tell you about that?"

About what? Her aunt hadn't told her much about him at all over the years, just as Sadie had apparently not told him about her.

"I don't know what you're referring to. I know you're a prominent attorney who was originally from California, and that's about all Sadie has told me."

"She also told you I'm brusque and demanding," he reminded, that quirky smile making a reappearance to let her know he found that amusing.

"And that you're brusque and demanding," she confirmed. "But nothing about what's wrong with my being here at eight tomorrow morning."

"I live in Georgetown, too. I'll pick you up at seven-thirty. I like to start work on the way in. It saves us going over what needs to be accomplished for the day when we both get here. So, seven-thirty," he repeated. "Sharp. Don't keep me waiting."

Since that sounded like a dismissal, Lucy stood.

"Seven-thirty. I'll be ready."

"And I have you until late tomorrow night."

Why did that sound like something that involved more than work?

She was probably just imagining it.

Or was he trying to charm her?

It didn't make any difference because she was absolutely going to ignore those flutters that were dancing around in her insides again in response.

"I'll even bring after-hours shoes," she said as if to convince him.

"Okay. Then we're squared away."

"But you will be looking for someone permanent to take my place? I really want to get into my freelance work at home before too long," she said to make sure they were clear.

"I have an employment agency on it as we speak."

"Good."

"Say hello to Sadie for me," Rand Colton said then.

"I will."

"If you're half the secretary she is, I'll be satisfied."

"I'm sure you'll be satisfied," Lucy said, mortified the moment the word was out of her mouth that she'd unconsciously put a lascivious spin on it. "With my work," she added in a hurry, compounding her error.

Rand Colton grinned at her this time. A full, delighted grin of glistening, perfect white teeth that let her know right then and there why he had so many women willing to spend time with him.

But he let her off the hook by crossing to the office

door to hold it open for her and saying a simple, "Seven-thirty."

Lucy fought the blush that was heating her cheeks and took her exit, unhappy that she also noticed the fresh, clean scent of his aftershave as she passed in front of him to leave.

"I'll tell Sadie you said hello," Lucy muttered just for something to say as she left the office.

But her encounter with Rand Colton didn't end then because he stayed in his doorway, watching her as she retraced her steps to the elevator. And when she hazarded a glance just before stepping into it, she found him still there, studying her.

But at least once the elevator doors closed she was alone and could breathe out the air she'd been unwittingly holding in her lungs.

It was going to be harder than she thought to work for Rand Colton, she realized on the way down from the twenty-third floor.

She could handle a difficult, demanding boss. But a difficult, demanding boss with gorgeous blue eyes, a body straight out of *Esquire*, charm, wit and even an unexpected sense of humor, who set off flutters in her stomach?

That was something else again.

Two

Rand had never needed much sleep. The next morning, as usual, he was awake before the November sun had made an appearance. It was his morning routine right after waking to pour himself a cup of coffee, grab the just-delivered *Washington Post* and climb back into bed to read it before he showered.

But this morning, current events weren't holding his interest. His gaze kept straying to the clock on his nightstand as if that would make time go faster.

He didn't understand why he was so eager to get to work. He hadn't felt that way in a long while now.

In fact, he hadn't felt particularly eager about anything in a while now.

There were family problems back home in Prosperino, California, and he'd tried to tell himself that was the cause. But the truth was that there was something about his own life that seemed to have taken a turn when he wasn't looking.

He didn't understand it, and he couldn't explain it. But in the last several months he'd lost some of the joy he'd found in things before. In his work. In his everyday life. In everything.

He still had the same intense drive to succeed, the same burning need to win his cases. That was just his nature—maybe because he was a firstborn. But he didn't feel that old desire to charge into his day anymore. Nor his after-hours activities either, whether it was dinner with a supermodel in town for a shoot, a party at the White House, a fund-raiser for one of his pet causes or a weekend in the country with a gorgeous woman. It was as if everything had become mundane to him. Even excelling at what he did or being on the A-list around town.

Yet here he was this morning, excited to get his day under way.

Why was that?

The day ahead of him was like any other one. He had calls to make, clients to see, briefs and motions to write, a court appearance after lunch and then more of the same when he got back. Then he had the evening working with Lucy Lowry to straighten up the messes left by the previous secretaries.

Lucy Lowry.

Thinking about her intensified his sense of eagerness.

His latest temporary secretary was causing it?

That couldn't be.

But there it was, irrefutably. What he was looking forward to today was seeing her again.

If that wasn't the oddest thing, he didn't know what was. He'd come away from their meeting yesterday thinking that *he* was who had really been interviewed. That *he'd* ended up being told how things were going to be run more than being the one to tell *her*. That *she'd* made the rules and left *him* to take it or leave it rather than the other way around. She was bossy and bold and outspoken.

So why was he so anxious to put himself in line for more of it?

She was great-looking, that was likely part of it. He was a sucker for a slender but curvy body with breasts that were just full enough. And that flawless ivory skin didn't hurt anything. Or that curly mahogany hair—she'd no doubt thought she'd camouflaged its natural seductiveness by trussing it up.

She had a pert little nose, too. Upturned at the end. That wasn't something he usually noticed, but for some reason he could picture it in his mind's eye as if he'd fashioned it himself.

Then there were her eyes. Wide eyes that offset her simmering sexuality with a more innocent, doelike quality. Sparkling, crystal-blue eyes the color of a clear mountain lake in springtime. They were alight with life, with vigor, energy and spunk. Plenty of spunk.

In fact, he realized as he watched the sunrise through the sliding doors that led from his bedroom onto the balcony, she had so much spunk she reminded him of the characters Katharine Hepburn had played in so many of her movies with Spencer Tracy. Beautiful, feisty, sharp, smart and able to hold her own with Tracy whether as a lawyer or a reporter or a business whiz.

That was Lucy Lowry—beautiful, feisty, sharp and smart.

And he couldn't seem to get the image of her out of his mind—any more than he could slow the increased beat of his heart every time she slipped into his head.

So what did that mean? That after fifteen minutes with her he was infatuated?

That was ridiculous.

He hadn't been infatuated-at-first-sight with anyone since his first year in college. He hadn't been particularly infatuated even after-first-sight with anyone for longer than he could remember. He enjoyed the company of the various women in his life. He looked forward to spending time with them, to everything they did together. But infatuated?

That was something else entirely.

That was like having a schoolboy crush and that wasn't something Rand Colton did.

But how else could he explain being so excited about going to work?

Maybe he was just glad to finally have someone competent onboard. Maybe the idea of getting his office in order again had just gone to his head.

Of course it would help if she hadn't put that five-o'clock stipulation on things, he thought, actually searching for something contrary to find in the situation.

What was that all about anyway? She'd been so adamant.

There had to be a man behind it, he decided. Some guy she was rushing home to, whether she admitted it or not.

But that possibility rankled Rand and again he looked for a reason.

He had so much work he needed taken care of—that was all. And there she was decreeing that her day would end at five o'clock on the dot no matter what.

Decreeing—that rubbed him wrong, too. And there'd been plenty of it. Plenty of decreeing and dictating. And big baby-blue eyes or no big baby-blue eyes, he didn't like it.

Any better than he liked the thought that she might be running to some other man....

Oh, brother, there was *that* again.

Some *other* man? As if he were involved with her and a boyfriend would be *another* man in her life?

"Maybe I've been working too hard," Rand muttered to himself, disgusted with his own train of thought.

Lucy Lowry was just one more in a string of women who had passed through his office since Sadie's retirement, he told himself reasonably. There had been a dozen before her, there would be more after her, and that was all there was to it. What she did outside the office and who she fraternized with were her own business and no concern of his.

And being eager to see her again this morning?

It was just...

Well, he didn't know what it was. But it wasn't infatuation.

He tossed aside his unread newspaper, set his coffee cup on the nightstand and got out of bed, feeling more agitated than eager now. Because the very idea that he might be interested in Lucy Lowry was too much to bear.

Women didn't come into his life and tell him what to do. And he sure as hell didn't like them if they did. He was only tolerating it in Lucy Lowry because he was in dire need of office help and Sadie had assured him he would get it from her niece.

Yet despite all his sternness with himself, all his reasoning and rationalizing, as he headed for the shower Lucy Lowry popped into his mind's eye again and he found himself wondering what that burnished hair of hers looked like down, falling in loose curls around her face.

And if she might wear it that way today...

Lucy's doorbell rang at precisely seven-twenty-nine.

She opened the door, expecting to find Rand Colton on the stoop and instead faced a stout, balding older man in a chauffeur's uniform.

She glanced beyond him at the long black Town

Car parked at the curb and assumed her boss was waiting there.

"I'll be right out," she informed the driver.

Then she closed the door again and went into the living room where Max sat on Sadie's lap, his teddy bear snuggled into the crook of one pajama-clad arm.

"Okay, buddy, I have to go. Remember what I told you last night—Aunt Sadie will bring you to day care later this morning when she goes to read to the kids. Until then you'll stay at her place. She's making you a special breakfast and I put your dinosaur videotape in your backpack so you can watch that if you want or you can watch cartoons. Then you'll come home with Aunt Sadie this afternoon and stay with her again. I probably won't be home before you go to bed but it's only this once and I'll call you today and again tonight. Got all that?"

Max nodded solemnly, more asleep than awake and seemingly unfazed by his mother's imminent departure.

"I'll miss you," Lucy told him.

"Miss you, too."

"Be a good boy."

Again the nod.

Lucy knew he'd be fine. She didn't have a doubt that Sadie would take good care of him or that he'd enjoy playing with kids his own age at the day care. She knew he did well with other children, that he made friends easily. But she still felt awful leaving him for such an extended amount of time.

It's only for today, she reminded herself.

And fast on that thought came one that had been popping into her head all through the last evening and again this morning like some kind of consolation prize—that she was spending the time away from her son with Rand Colton.

She didn't want that to be something that could brighten her spirits. But for some reason it was. Some reason she didn't even want to think about, let alone analyze.

"Kiss," she demanded of her son.

An instant, impish grin tugged at the corner of Max's mouth just before he planted a wet one on her cheek. Then he turned his face for her to do the same to him.

"I'm taking the Triceratops to day care with me," he informed her in the meantime.

"Okay, but you know the deal. You have to share."

"Then maybe I better take the Tyrannosaurus, too."

Max said that as if it were serious business, which, to him, dinosaurs were.

"Have a nice day." She ruffled his hair as she said goodbye to her aunt, then forced herself to walk out the door.

"You have a good day, too," Sadie called after her.

The big black Lincoln Town Car outside had windows too darkly tinted to see through, yet knowing Rand was in that back seat made Lucy's pulse pick up more speed with each step that drew her nearer.

She wanted to believe it was nothing but first-day jitters. But she knew better. This had more to do with the man himself. And as much as she wished she could deny that fact, she couldn't.

There had been something about their brief meeting the day before that had caused him to stick in her mind vividly. Images of his tall, lean-but-muscular body, of his handsome face, even of his big hands, had kept her company all through the night.

Something about their brief meeting had caused her to wake up earlier than necessary this morning with a desire to dress just so for their coming day and evening together, inspiring her to wear her best suit, a pale blue cashmere that buttoned in a diagonal from her right shoulder to her left hip. It had been an extremely expensive birthday gift from her aunt that she saved for only the most important workdays.

And worst of all, there had been something about her brief meeting with Rand Colton that had caused her to look forward to today as if it were some kind of special occasion she'd been waiting for her whole life.

He's your boss, she reminded herself firmly. Not to mention that he was arrogant and irascible. And that she wasn't interested.

But still, as his driver got out and hurried around the car, a twitter of excitement danced across the surface of her skin at the imminence of seeing Rand Colton again. And no amount of telling herself that sense of excitement was completely uncalled-for made any difference.

When the driver opened the door for her, she got her first view of Rand. Or at least of his profile.

His dark, dark hair was impeccably combed, his face clean-shaven, and the scent of his aftershave wafted enticingly out to her.

He wasn't wearing a suit coat to cover his pristine white dress shirt, complete with French cuffs and cuff links of brushed gold. Against the stark whiteness of the shirt he wore a mauve silk tie Windsor-knotted at his throat. His suit pants were a rich wool that were not quite black and not quite gray but somewhere between the two. He looked better than any man had a right to that early in the morning.

But Lucy tried not to notice.

"Thank you," she muttered to the driver as she slipped into the back seat.

Rand was writing something on a sheet of paper braced by a leather-bound notebook. The notebook was propped against a massive thigh that was raised with the aid of his ankle perched atop the opposite knee.

He didn't look up as Lucy got in and the driver closed the door behind her. He didn't even say good morning.

Neither did she. Instead she said, "You're from California and you don't know how to drive?"

"Of course I know *how* to drive," he answered, still not looking up from what he was doing. "But I like living in Georgetown and I *don't* like taking the Metro into the city."

Oh no, no public transportation for His Nibs...

"Besides," he went on, "we can get a surprising lot of work done on the way into the office if someone else is behind the wheel and fighting traffic. So yes, I own a car, but I also invest in a service that provides this car and driver."

He continued to write at a breakneck pace and apparently didn't intend to waste any more time on small talk because he said, "You'll find paper and pen in the pocket behind the seat. Take this down."

And so Lucy's day began.

From that moment on she barely had time to even notice Rand the man. He was like working with an excessively efficient machine. It took everything she had to keep up with him whether he was rattling off the perfect letter or having her jot down notes on his train of thought in preparation for writing a brief, or ordering her to fix his coffee, or to get a client on the phone or bring him a file.

He had the most rapid-fire mind—and mouth to go with it—that she'd ever encountered. No wonder he'd run through a succession of secretaries, Lucy thought more than once during the day. He was almost superhuman and what he really needed was two or three secretaries to meet all his needs.

Not that Lucy missed a step, because she didn't. In fact, matching him movement for movement became a challenge to her, and once she'd met that challenge, she one-upped him by anticipating several requests before he actually made them. Even though the job and the pace were not what she would have opted to do every day for the rest of her life, she found it all exhilarating. She found *him* exhilarating, if she were honest with herself or had had the time to ponder it.

She did manage to sneak in a phone call to Max while Rand was in court, but beyond that the day flew by. Before she knew it, it was nearly 6:00 p.m. and they switched gears to tackle what Rand called the mess in the library—stacks of papers and files that previous secretaries had obviously set aside to deal with after the maelstrom of Rand's workday and then never gotten back to.

But the evening's work was actually a nice change. After hours her sometimes-hard-to-take boss grew much less intense. Off came the exquisitely tailored suit coat he'd worn from the moment he'd gotten out of the car that morning, joined over a chair-back by his tie. Then he opened the collar button of his hardly wrinkled shirt and rolled his sleeves up to his elbows, exposing a thick neck and forearms so sinewy any construction worker would have been proud of them.

"Get out those comfortable shoes you said you were bringing," he advised Lucy as he led the way to the room he less formally referred to as the research room.

Rand was still all business as they passed the evening going through the stacks of papers. He checked each sheet to make sure what it contained and where it belonged, then handed it to Lucy, telling her which file to put it in.

It was a monotonous task that didn't allow for conversation as Rand concentrated on what he was doing. But Lucy found herself waiting almost breathlessly for each of those silences to be broken by the deep tones of a voice so rich it could have come from a jazz singer in a smoky New Orleans bar.

When all the papers were tucked neatly into the files, Lucy excused herself for a bathroom break and used her cell phone to call Max and bid him good-night. By the time she returned to the office Rand had transferred all the files to the file room where they spent the remainder of the evening sifting through the deep drawers of the cabinets to put the files away.

She was surprised to find Rand joining her in that portion of the job. Making sure the papers got into the correct files had required his participation, but finding the right slot for them was certainly not something he needed to attend to. Yet there he was, doing just that, right alongside her.

It was nice, Lucy admitted reluctantly. Nice to see that no job was too small for his attention. Rand Colton might be a bear to work for but he didn't demand any less of himself than he did of anyone else, and somehow that seemed to cushion the weight of his heavy expectations.

By ten o'clock Lucy was beat and glad when they finally finished.

Even Rand seemed worn out as he raised long arms above his head, flexed his broad shoulders and stretched toward the ceiling.

"Okay, enough is enough," he said to the accompaniment of his back cracking. "That was quite a day's work."

"No argument here," Lucy agreed, rubbing at a crick in her neck.

"I didn't even let you stop for dinner."

"I didn't let you stop for dinner either," she countered with a small laugh.

"I think I owe you that much. What if we hit the diner around the corner before we go back to Georgetown? My treat for a job well done."

That was all the invitation sounded like, too. It wasn't as if he were asking her out on a date or even angling for that. Which, for no good reason, felt slightly demoralizing to Lucy.

But it was the way things *should* be, she told herself. He was just her boss, she was just his secretary. They'd put in over fourteen hours of work and he was trying to reward her for it. That was all there was to it.

Still, though, she knew she should decline the offer. Despite the fact that Sadie was baby-sitting and had long since put Max to bed, Lucy knew she should go home.

But she *was* hungry.

And Max would be asleep and wouldn't know the difference if she were gone another hour.

"What do you say?" Rand urged when she hadn't answered immediately.

"Nothing fancy?" she heard herself ask right in the middle of giving herself reasons why it wasn't a good idea to fraternize with the boss.

"It's a diner. Definitely nothing fancy. And if you think I can protect you out on the mean streets of

Washington, we can walk there, eat and then call for the car so we don't interrupt whatever sporting event Frank's watching while he waits for us to page him.''

Frank was Rand's driver and was apparently on-call. Lucy thought it was yet another surprise to find Rand considerate of the other man. And as for trusting that Rand could protect her on a late-night walk anywhere, it only took one look at the size of him, at the confidence in his comportment, to judge the notion of not being safe with him a joke.

"A walk would be good," she agreed. "I could use the fresh air."

"Let's do it, then."

Within minutes they were down the elevator and out in the cold, crisp evening.

"This way," Rand said with a nod to his right as he pulled on leather gloves the same charcoal color as the knee-length camel hair overcoat he wore.

Lucy had buttoned up her own black wool overcoat and also took gloves from her pockets as they headed off down the street that was still alive with people and traffic.

Neither Lucy nor Rand said much along the way. Lucy could only assume that he was doing the same thing she was doing—winding down.

The diner around the corner was just a hole-in-the-wall on the bottom floor of the office building abutting Rand's. It had booths around the perimeter and counter-seating behind which was a cut-out in the wall that opened to the kitchen where orders and plates were exchanged.

The restaurant was about half-full and Rand led the way to a vacant booth.

''Workin' late tonight are ya, counselor?'' the waitress called to them from behind the cash register a split second after they sat down.

She was an older woman with her hair cut in a man's crew cut and a large black mole below her left eye. Lucy noticed as she approached their table that she was dressed in the classic Liberty-green waitress dress, white apron and white nurse's shoes that might have come right out of a diner from the 1950s.

Rand answered her greeting as if they were well-acquainted and ordered two Blue Plate Specials before so much as consulting Lucy.

When the waitress left he said, ''The Blue Plate is pot roast, potatoes, salad and rolls. At this time of night you don't want anything off the grill. It hasn't been cleaned since dawn and the food that comes off it is pretty bad. I should have warned you before we got here but since I didn't I couldn't do it in front of Gail. She's part-owner and would have been insulted.''

The offense Lucy had taken at not being asked what she wanted to eat abated with that explanation. She could hardly fault him for looking out for both her palate and the waitress's feelings. So she decided to just go with the flow rather than make an issue of Rand Colton's high-handedness.

Gail returned with water and asked if they wanted coffee.

This time Rand raised his eyebrows at Lucy, waiting for her to answer for herself.

"I'll have herbal tea."

"I'll have iced tea," Rand added.

They'd settled their coats and gloves on the booth seats beside them and so there they were, face-to-face, with nothing to distract them. And although the view was grand since Rand looked every bit as terrific as he had to start the day, it was unnerving to have those penetrating eyes of his studying her as if she were a painting on a museum wall.

"How did you get from California to Washington D.C.?" Lucy asked just to get the conversational ball rolling.

"I was here a couple of times as a kid. To visit my father. He was a Senator when I was pretty young and my mother brought us here to see him. It was so exciting it stuck with me. Then I spent the summer after my first year of law school here, interning at a think tank, which basically means I spent twelve hours a day, six days a week, researching arcane case law for one of the resident thinkers. I still found the city exciting, though, and since it seemed like a good place to make my mark, after I graduated I decided to put out my shingle here."

"Is your family still in California?"

He raised the chiseled chin that had been freshly shaved during Lucy's bathroom break to call home. "Hacienda del Alegria—that's the old homestead in Prosperino. My folks and an assortment of siblings and almost-siblings are still there, yes."

"Siblings and almost-siblings?"

"My family has a colorful history when it comes to kids. There were six biological kids and a slew of adopted and foster kids my parents took in over the years."

"Really?" That was interesting, especially given Rand's stand against his secretary having children. It had left Lucy with the impression that he might not like kids, that maybe he'd been an only child himself.

"Did you resent your parents taking in foster children?" she asked as their meals were served, thinking that maybe resentment had turned him sour on the subject.

"Did I *resent* it?" he repeated as he liberally salted his food. "No, why would you think that?"

Lucy tasted a small bite of the pot roast, judged it more than edible, and then said, "You're so against single mothers as secretaries."

"Just because it interferes with work. I like kids well enough and I certainly never resented my folks giving a home to foster kids."

"How did your parents start that? Had they done it before having a family of their own and just kept it up afterward? Or had they already had all of you and still wanted more?" she asked then, as they both settled into eating.

"It didn't start until after they had five of us. When I was thirteen one of my brothers, Michael, was killed by a drunk driver while he and the other twin, Drake, were out riding their bicycles. It was a rough time after that. My father in particular went into a deep depression. My mother got the idea of taking in kids without homes when my dad confided some things about his own growing-up years. The suggestion struck a chord in him. In fact, it was sort of a turning point for him. He realized that family was the most important thing to him and decided to give up politics and focus on his home life. Since then they've become pretty well-known for taking in stray kids. In '91 someone even left a baby on their doorstep.''

"Wow. They must be great parents.''

"I'd say they're pretty normal. They had their strong points and their weak points like most parents. Not that I'm complaining. I had a terrific childhood. But I hated it when my dad was here and we were all in California. It was lousy having an absentee parent. Maybe that's part of the single-mother-secretary thing. When you have kids, you need to be able to be there for them. The way I work makes that impossible, which is why I don't have kids myself and why it's important that my secretary not have them either. Something has to give and I believe when you're a parent, that ultimately has to come first.''

"So no parents for secretaries,'' Lucy summed up.

"In my office, anyway. I'm devoted to my work and I need my secretary to—''

"Be devoted to you.''

"I was going to say that I need my secretary to be as dedicated as I am.''

"To the exclusion of his or her own life.''

Rand had the good grace to laugh and flinch at once. "You're really hard on me.''

"Not as hard as you are in your demands of a secretary. I guess you can dish it out but you can't take it."

He eyed her with a combination of amusement and wariness as he flipped open his cell phone and paged his driver to tell him where they could be picked up since they'd both finished their meals.

Then, without skipping a beat, he said, "I just think people need to prioritize. If you have kids, you need to accommodate them, arrange your life around them and avoid demanding jobs. If you have a demanding job—"

"Or boss."

"Or boss. You shouldn't have kids because they get shortchanged."

"Is everything so black and white for you?"

"Not everything. But this is."

"So no kids for your secretary and no kids for you."

"Exactly."

"Ever?" Lucy asked as Rand tossed two twenty-dollar bills onto the table without having seen the check.

"I don't know. I'm not sure I could ever do what it takes to be a father. Maybe someday. But a far-off someday. Like when I retire."

"Retire? You want to have kids after you retire?" Lucy said, laughing at the notion as they both put on their coats.

"I plan to retire fairly young."

"Not young enough to wait until then to have kids, I'll bet."

"What makes you think so?"

"You're crazed. You won't be able to even slow down anytime soon, let alone retire."

"Then I guess it's no kids for me."

"Seems like a shame," Lucy observed as she got into the back seat of the Town Car when it pulled up outside the diner.

"Why is that?"

"From the way you talk I can tell family is important to you." That made him all the more appealing, something Lucy didn't want to acknowledge to herself.

"Family is important to me. That's the point. If you have a family, they have to be the *most* important thing in your life."

"And instead your job fills the bill?"

"Completely."

"Your job can't curl up on your lap to read Dr. Seuss or melt your heart with a smile or tie your shoes when you're too old to do it yourself."

"I like my job," he defended.

"Enough to exclude everything else?"

He smiled the most wicked smile she'd ever seen. "It excludes kids. No one said it excluded everything else," he said with a tone full of innuendo.

Lucy rolled her eyes. "I give up." Although in truth it wasn't their arguing she was so willing to throw in the towel on. It was that the innuendo was too scintillating to be safe for her any longer. Especially when that wicked grin had an incredibly heady effect on her.

"And here you were holding your own so well," he said as if he were disappointed that she wasn't continuing to challenge him.

Somehow when Lucy had gotten into the car she hadn't slid completely to the opposite end of the seat. And somehow when Rand had followed her in, he'd slid a little more toward the center than he'd needed to. Lucy hadn't noticed it before, but now she realized that they were only separated by about six inches. Plus Rand was turned at a slight angle and had his arm stretched across the seat back so near to her she became aware of his coat sleeve brushing her nape.

It all worked together to allow him to look directly at her. To study her with a warmth in his eyes that made her want to take off her coat.

Then he said, "Tell your aunt thanks for me."

"For what? Providing an adequate sparring partner?"

He laughed lightly. "Well, for that—I always enjoy a good debate. But also for sending me the best secretary I've had since she left."

It flashed through Lucy's mind to say he hadn't *had* her, but she caught herself before she uttered the words.

What was she doing? she asked herself. Was she really on the verge of flirting with him? Was one long workday and a Blue Plate Special all it took to drop her guard?

But it wasn't easy keeping her guard up when the

man only inches from her was so astonishingly handsome, so charming, so stimulating, so sexy.

And it didn't help matters that there he was, searching her face as if he'd just made some discovery in her that he could hardly believe himself, his expression full of admiration, of appreciation for more than a job well-done. For something that appeared far more personal. Far more flattering.

Then his eyes honed in on hers, delving into them, making her feel even hotter still and suddenly causing her to think about kissing. About him kissing her. About her kissing him back...

It would be a mistake, she told herself sternly. *A huge mistake.*

Yet her mouth went dry with the very notion. Her mind raced with curiosity about how those wonderful male lips would feel pressed to hers. Would they be parted? Would his tongue tease her lips into parting, too? What would he taste like? Would his mouth, his tongue, be as agile as his mind? As forceful as his personality? As powerful as his sex appeal?

Where would he put his hands? Those big, adept, blunt-fingered hands she'd been mesmerized by all day and evening. Would they be warm? Tender or strong?

Would she forget everything in one perfect moment of bliss that would make everything right with the world? One brief, perfect moment she could lose herself in the way she hadn't in so, so long?

Or would it be more than one moment? Would it

go on and on until her lips were numb and every ounce of her was alive with wanting…?

Lucy realized suddenly that she'd actually leaned forward. Just a hair. But maybe enough to be sending a signal that relayed what was going through her mind. A signal she knew better than to give.

She sat up straighter. She leaned back ever so slightly but enough to overcompensate if she actually had leaned forward in anticipation of being kissed.

"So, what time on Monday?" she blurted out, her effort to sound businesslike sounding abrasive to her own ears.

But all Rand Colton did was smile. A small, secret smile that made her think he knew exactly what had gone through her mind. Knew exactly what she was fighting. Knew exactly what his impact on her entailed.

"I think we've earned a later start. I'll pick you up at eight instead of seven-thirty."

The car came to a stop at the curb in front of her house just then and Lucy silently thanked the fates for that bit of mercy.

She opened the door before the driver could put the car in park and do it for her. "Monday at eight," she repeated much too brightly.

"Lucy?" Rand said to stall her escape.

"Hmm?" she responded over her shoulder, one foot already on the sidewalk outside.

"Thanks for today and tonight. If you'd consider taking the job on a permanent basis, it'd be yours."

The job.

So he hadn't lost sight for even a moment of the fact that they were boss and secretary. Only she had.

"No thanks," she said curtly. "In fact I'll see if I can't light a fire under that employment agency Monday to arrange some interviews right away." Before the fire he seemed to have unwittingly and without effort lit inside her singed her for real.

"Good night," she said then, getting completely out of the car. "Thanks for dinner."

He acknowledged her gratitude with another lift of his chin before he said, "See you Monday."

Lucy fled the car, leaving the door to be closed by Frank and fighting the impression that there had been some sort of promise in Rand's parting "See you Monday."

It was only her imagination, she told herself. Just as all those thoughts of him kissing her had only been in her imagination.

And as she let herself into her town house she couldn't be sure which presented more danger to her—her own wayward thoughts or the potent appeal of Rand Colton.

Three

Rand Colton was on Lucy's mind. He'd been there when she'd gone to bed Friday night, he'd been there the moment she woke up Saturday morning, he'd been there all weekend and he was still there Monday morning even before her alarm went off, as she lay in bed.

It was very troubling.

Not only couldn't she stop thinking about him, but her thoughts...

Very troubling, indeed.

She'd had no business thinking about him kissing her. *Vividly* thinking about him kissing her. No business at all. She had to be out of her mind.

He was her boss. He was a workaholic over-achiever who didn't even want a single mother working for him, let alone in any more personal role. And she had better not lose sight of it just because he was a fascinating man.

And he was that, she had to admit.

A fascinating man who also happened to be great-looking, more man than she'd ever met and a brilliant attorney—the kind she'd wanted to be herself before fate had stepped in and made that impossible.

Rand Colton was a fascinating man who also happened to be charming and suave and sophisticated, with a good sense of humor and an admirable strength in his convictions.

What are you, his biggest fan? she asked herself.

Maybe he should have hired her to do his public relations work instead of his secretarial work.

Oh, yeah, her thoughts were troubling, all right.

She'd just met him and here she was ticking off enough attributes to make him sound like Superman.

It just wouldn't do.

But then none of the places her thoughts were leading her would do.

She had enough on her plate taking care of Max and trying to support them both, she reminded herself. She didn't have time for daydreams like she'd fallen into all weekend. Let alone time for a relationship or a romance—even if a relationship or a romance was what Rand Colton was offering.

And it wasn't.

So why was she having such a hard time getting him off her mind when she knew better?

Maybe it was a result of deprivation. There was no

denying that she was a young, vital woman who hadn't had a date in almost five years. And not only that, she also spent most of her time in the company of a four-year-old. It wasn't even unusual for her to go days without so much as speaking to another adult, especially since quitting her job at the Bar Association library a month ago to make this move to Washington.

So she could make an argument for having been deprived of contact with people her own age, along with being deprived of contact with a man.

Given that, it only made sense that a few hours out in the adult world with someone like Rand Colton would go to her head.

But that was all there was to it, she tried to convince herself. A rebound effect of social and interpersonal deprivation.

And when the man she was out in the adult world with was a man like Rand Colton—a man impossible for any woman not to find attractive—of course she was attracted. Of course her mind was doing some natural wandering. Some natural wondering. Some fantasizing.

But fantasizing was harmless enough, she reasoned. As long as she didn't act on any of it.

And as long as he didn't know what was going on. Or did he?

She hoped not. But she *had* escaped her own kissing ruminations to find him smiling that smile at her, as if he'd been able to read her every thought like closed-captioning at the bottom of a television screen.

No, that was just silly. He could have had any number of things on his mind to cause that smile.

Still, he'd been looking at her, studying her, which meant the smile might have been an indication that he liked what he saw.

Now *that* was a dangerous possibility, Lucy realized, annoyed with her once-again-wandering thoughts.

Worse than being attracted to him was the idea that he might have been attracted to her.

She didn't need that.

Oh sure, it would be a nice boost to her ego. But look what the last boost to her ego had gotten her— Max and raising him alone.

Only this time she wouldn't be able to say she hadn't been warned about what the man was all about. Rand Colton had made himself perfectly clear. No kids. Period.

"So stop thinking about him," she whispered to herself in the pre-dawn darkness of her bedroom as if the spoken word would have more impact.

She really had to stop thinking about how much she'd enjoyed working with him—despite how demanding he was and how high were his expectations.

She had to stop thinking about how much she'd enjoyed bantering with him, debating the child issue, having dinner with him.

She had to stop thinking about cobalt-blue eyes and mile-wide shoulders, and thighs that tested the limits of his impeccably tailored trousers and hands that could cup the entire back of her head against the pressure of a kiss....

"Stop it, stop it, stop it!" she said more forcefully.

She honestly did not want to be thinking the things she was thinking. She honestly didn't want to be attracted to any man. And she honestly didn't want any boosts to her ego that could make her vulnerable again.

Yes, Max had come out of that vulnerability and she adored her son. No, she wouldn't change anything that would mean he wasn't in her life.

But she couldn't afford to risk anything that might make history repeat itself, either. She couldn't afford it financially or emotionally.

Max's father had hurt her terribly. He hurt her all over again every time Max asked why he didn't have a dad like other kids did.

Lucy would never willingly open up herself or Max to more of the grief that had already been caused by a man whose life was clearly set on one course. A man who had no interest, no inclination, no intention whatsoever of altering that course to accommodate a woman with a child.

"So get your head out of the clouds, Lucy," she told herself as her alarm went off.

Because getting involved with a man like Rand Colton once was enough. In fact it was absolutely, unequivocally more than enough.

Once again Sadie was taking Max to day care later in the morning and had come to sit with the little boy

when it was time for Lucy to leave. But today Lucy
made sure to say her goodbyes ahead of time so that
the moment Rand's driver rang her doorbell she was
ready. In fact she nearly rushed him in her hurry to
get out.

But this morning when Frank opened the rear car
door for her it was to an empty back seat.

One glance there and another to the tall, stoic driver
prompted an explanation.

"Mr. Colton had an early breakfast meeting. I've
already taken him into the city. We aren't to go directly to the office either. You'll find a list of things
he wants you to do today in the pocket behind the
passenger's seat."

"He didn't say—" Lucy cut herself off, hating the
confused, disappointed tone her voice had taken, as
if she and Rand had had some sort of private plans
he'd changed without telling her, leaving his driver
to do the dirty work. In truth, he owed her no explanation and she should have been grateful he'd still
sent his driver for her.

"Fine," she amended in her best businesslike de-
meanor before the driver saw what she was really
feeling. Then she got into the car as if she'd been
born to it and didn't wait for Frank to close the door
before searching for the note Rand had left her.

Not that it was actually a note. There was nothing
written on the sheet of paper she unfolded but a to-
do list. No warm greeting. No "It slipped my mind
Friday night that I had these things for you to do."
No "I'm sorry for not warning you that you're on

your own today.'' Nothing but one task after another
that she was to take care of.

*He doesn't owe you any more than that. You're just
his secretary,* she lectured herself, trying not to let it
bother her as she read the list.

1. Pick up dry cleaning
2. Make enclosed bank deposit
3. Go to florist to hand-pick three arrangements
and sign cards: Happy Birthday Deidre. Rand /
Congratulations on your promotion, Bunny. I
had a great time celebrating. Rand / Thanks for
a wonderful evening, Veronica. Rand

There were other items on the list but she was too
struck to read them in any detail. Instead she reread
the first three things, the third several times, feeling
her pique rise higher with each reading.

What did he think she was, his handmaiden? His
servant? His social secretary? Laundry and bank de-
posits and flowers to girlfriends. *Girlfriends!* Plural.
Deidre and Bunny and Veronica.

Did he imagine himself to be some kind of playboy
potentate? Dishing out orders without so much as a
please or thank-you. Forcing her to write his love mis-
sives to other women at the same time she was supposed to play wife with his cleaning and banking?

What nerve. What gall. What—

What was she doing getting mad?

Lucy put the brakes on the things going through
her mind, on the anger that was gaining momentum.

You're just his secretary, she reminded herself yet again.

Granted, she hadn't assumed the job would entail his personal errands. That wasn't what she had agreed to and it also wasn't something she *would* have agreed to. But that wasn't all that was making her mad. Every time she read that third item on the list and saw those other women's names, she could feel her blood boil.

And why? she asked herself.

Because she was jealous.

She abhorred the very idea. But there it was—unwarranted, unwanted jealousy. Jealousy she had no right to. No reason for. No rational excuse for.

You're just his secretary!

Her aunt had told her Rand was a man-about-town. But somehow Lucy hadn't taken that into consideration. Why should she have? It didn't have anything to do with her.

Except that one day of working for him and she was feeling possessive.

It was insane.

She had no business feeling that way.

Social and interpersonal deprivation or not, this was uncalled for.

On the other hand, she thought as she fought to regain some control, some equilibrium, maybe this was just the wake-up call she needed today. Maybe it was good to have the evidence right under her nose that Rand was the man he was. That he wasn't some uncomplicated, ordinary nice guy who might break down her barriers to convince her that she should allow him into Max's and her life.

No, what she had there in front of her was written proof that Rand Colton was an entirely different breed. A breed that juggled women and didn't have time for kids.

And she was just his secretary. His *temporary* secretary.

And she'd better not forget it.

But still, as the car stopped at the curb in front of the dry cleaners for her first chore of the day, she couldn't untie the knot in the pit of her stomach left by that renewed knowledge that she and Rand Colton were on two very different tracks.

That she was on the mommy track with Max.

And that Rand was on the fast track with Deidre, Bunny and Veronica.

"So, Max, have you told your mom what you want to be when you grow up?"

Sadie had invited Max and Lucy to dinner that night and while she and Lucy put together a salad, Max sat at the kitchen table coloring in his new coloring book.

"No, not yet," Max answered.

"Today's story at day care was about what to be when you grow up and then everybody got a turn talking about it," Sadie explained to Lucy.

"Last I heard you wanted to be a fighter pilot or a policeman," Lucy said.

"Not anymore," Max informed her matter-offactly, without looking up from his coloring. "Now I'm gonna be a pail-intologer. That's the guy who works at the moo-seum putting the dinosaurs' bones together. And some of the times I'm gonna sing songs with a guitar."

"A paleontologist and a rock star, huh?" Lucy mused.

"He sang us a song, too," Sadie contributed. Then, barely suppressing a laugh, she added, "Maybe later he can perform again. I think you ought to see it."

"Last Saturday he was enthralled with an old Elvis Presley movie on TV. Don't tell me I'm raising a little Elvis impersonator."

"Forget the college fund. You'd better start saving for the sparkling suits, big belt buckles and wig," her aunt advised. "Max does 'Blue Suede Shoes' like a pro. He had every teacher and aide rolling in the aisles. And if you think he's shy, think again."

Max was listening to this exchange even though he still hadn't stopped coloring, and a grin stretched from ear to ear at his reviews.

Lucy was about to ask to see him sing when the doorbell rang.

"Our other guest," Sadie said as she wiped her hands on a dish towel and headed for the door.

"I didn't know there was going to be another guest, did you?" Lucy asked Max.

He nodded his head. "I helped Aunt Sadie set the dining room table."

Not that Lucy minded that someone else would be joining them. She was always happy to meet new people, especially now that she needed to cultivate a Washington circle of friends.

But then she heard a man's voice and froze.

It wasn't just any man's voice. It was the deep tones of a voice she recognized instantly—Rand Colton.

And panic replaced the pleasant prospect of meeting someone new.

Lucy hadn't told her aunt about Rand's no-kids dictate. Or that she hadn't confessed that she had Max. It just hadn't come up.

No, that wasn't exactly true.

The truth was, Lucy hadn't brought it up because she was so chagrined at having kept Max a secret. And since the job was only temporary, she'd just chosen to keep that under wraps when it came to her aunt.

It hadn't occurred to her that it would backfire by Sadie getting them all together.

"Here they are," Sadie was saying as she led the way into the warm kitchen, redolent with the scent of roasting chicken. "My two darlings. Lucy and Max. I don't suppose you've met Max yet, have you, Rand?"

There wasn't time to make a run for it. There wasn't even time to think of a face-saving excuse or some glib quip. Instead Lucy looked up from the salad she was dressing to find her handsome boss taking in the whole domestic scene, his expression confused as his gaze went to Max while Sadie made the introduction.

And what was even worse, Max seemed to fall in

love at first sight with the big man. The little boy's blue eyes sparkled and his smile showed pure delight.

"I'm coloring a Tyrannosaurus. He ate other dinosaurs."

"Did he? I didn't know that," Rand answered amiably enough. But then he turned a much more cloudy expression to Lucy as he added, "But then there are a lot of things I don't know."

Sadie seemed to pick up on the tension between Lucy and Rand but she kept up a good front. "I've opened a bottle of wine. Will you have a glass?" she asked Rand then. "Dinner is just about ready."

"I think a glass of wine might be a good idea. Maybe it'll have a calming effect," he said pointedly, still letting his gaze bore into Lucy with the heat of ten lasers.

She drew herself up, pulling back her shoulders, straightening her spine, holding her head high. Just as Rand had his own life that was none of her business, her life was none of his. And she was *not* going to cower or sulk or try to deny the fact that yes, she did have a son. A son she loved to death. A son she was proud of.

"Go wash your hands for dinner, Max," Lucy told the little boy gently, meeting Rand's stormy eyes with a defiant gaze of her own to let him know he could take this turn of events or leave them, that she couldn't care less.

Sadie poured Rand a glass of wine, making small talk that he responded to while still staring daggers at Lucy.

Then Max returned from the bathroom, slipped his hand into Rand's as if it were something he'd done a million times before, and said, "Come on. I'll show you where to sit. You can be by me."

"Thank you," Rand said to both Max and Sadie at once as he accepted the wineglass with his free hand before letting the child take him into the dining room.

He earned points with Lucy for not rejecting the handholding or the invitation to sit with her son, no matter how mad he might be at her.

The moment Max and Rand were out of earshot Sadie sidled up next to Lucy and whispered, "He didn't know about Max?"

"It was an underlying condition of the job that I not be a single mother. He said he was sick of dealing with them and all the complications that came with them. He said having kids interfered with work. He assumed I didn't have any and I didn't inform him otherwise."

"Oh, dear."

"It's okay. As long as he's nice to Max tonight, he can do what he wants about me tomorrow," Lucy assured her aunt, casting a glance in the direction of the dining room where she could hear her son regaling her boss with his career plans.

Rand was nice to Max, though. All evening. More than nice, he was actually good with the little boy who had been stricken by a sudden case of hero worship and seemed to have made it his goal to charm the object of it.

For her part, Lucy let her son have free rein. Ordinarily she would have attempted to keep him in check so he didn't monopolize an adult evening, but tonight she didn't. Tonight she wanted Rand to see that she doted on Max, that she wasn't ashamed of him in any way.

As a result, Max was the entertainment of the evening. He told his dinosaur stories and demonstrated dinosaurs stalking other dinosaurs. He did his full repertoire of knock-knock jokes and then he sang "Blue Suede Shoes"—complete with hip-wiggling gyrations, air guitar, and a curled lip at the end.

For his part, Rand didn't seem to mind. In fact he held up his own side of the conversation with Max, posing questions as if the little boy were the resident expert—which he actually was.

Rand told a few of his own knock-knock jokes, surprising both Lucy and Sadie that he knew them, and laughed and clapped as heartily as Lucy and Sadie at the end of "Blue Suede Shoes."

It was all a relief to Lucy because no matter how angry Rand was at her—and it was still clear she was in trouble with him—at least he didn't take it out on her son.

By eight o'clock Max was getting overtired and slap-happy so Lucy announced that it was time to go home.

After a few protests, Max went to stand directly in front of Rand and held out his right hand for Rand to shake.

"It was nice to meet you," the little boy said like a seasoned businessman.

Rand accepted Max's hand with the same decorum. "It was nice to meet you, too."

Max beamed as if he'd been granted the best compliment in the world and then ran to where his mother waited for him at the front door.

But Lucy couldn't go without posing the first question she'd aimed directly at Rand all evening. "Should I come to work tomorrow?" she asked with a high note of challenge in her tone.

"The car will be here at seven-thirty," he answered, but dourly enough to leave Lucy wondering if he just wanted to berate her in his office before he fired her.

"Seven-thirty," she repeated.

Then she thanked Sadie for dinner, urged Max to do the same and left.

But if she thought her stress for the evening was over when she stepped out into the cold night air to cross the few feet of sidewalk to her own town house next door, she was mistaken.

Because an hour later, just as she was coming down the stairs from reading Max to sleep and tucking him in, there was a sharp knock on her front door that she somehow knew didn't bode well.

She took a deep breath and decided if Rand had changed his mind and decided to fire her tonight instead of tomorrow she'd just as soon get it over with.

So, with her shoulders once again squared, she

crossed the small entryway at the foot of the stairs and opened the door.

Sure enough, Rand was outside, leaning one shoulder against the jamb as if she'd kept him waiting, his arms crossed over his expansive chest.

She hadn't taken notice of what he had on before, but she did now. Tan slacks, navy blue blazer, navy blue V-neck sweater over a cream-colored shirt with the collar button left open. As good as he looked in his expensive suits, he looked even better in the more casual attire.

Except that his handsome face was still a thundercloud.

"Change of plans?" she asked, not bothering with a greeting.

"Just thought I'd stop by before I went home and find out why you lied to me," he answered, his voice even deeper than usual and so low there was no chance of it waking Max. So low it was even more ominous than had he been shouting.

But even though he wasn't likely to wake the neighborhood, she still didn't want to do this on the front stoop so she stepped aside and formally invited him in.

When he was inside she closed the door and led the way into the living room to the left of the foyer. It was the one portion of the house that had no boxes left to be unpacked and the furniture positioned where it would stay.

Lucy went to the bean-pot lamp on the antique oak

end table beside her overstuffed plaid sofa and turned it on.

"Would you like to sit?" she asked.

But when she turned to see where Rand had landed she found him the same way he'd been outside—leaning a shoulder against the archway between the entry and the living room, his arms once again over his chest, his weight slung on one hip and his expression an expectant, direly solemn mask as he waited for an answer to his question.

So Lucy cut to the chase.

"I didn't lie to you," she said, taking her own stand behind the overstuffed chair that matched the sofa. "I just didn't tell you about Max. As long as my being his mother doesn't interfere with the job you're paying me to do, he's none of your business. And since I haven't heard any complaints, I assume my having a child hasn't caused a problem, has it?"

Rand ignored the challenge in her tone. In fact, he seemed to ignore what she'd said. "I don't like being lied to."

"No one does. But you left it up to me, and I just opted to leave out the fact that I'm a parent."

"Omission is still a lie in my book."

"Well, in *my* book it's an omission. And had you not come to dinner tonight, you would never have known there'd been one because I don't let Max interfere with my work. As you've seen for yourself."

"I need you later than five in the evening and you won't stay so you can get home to him. What do you call that?"

"I call it a nine-hour workday if it starts at seventhirty and I only take half an hour for lunch. I think that's sufficient."

"Not if I need you longer."

Why had that sounded more personal than professional? Maybe she was just imagining it.

"I'm not your permanent secretary, remember? I'm just the fill-in. You can stipulate whatever you like when you hire someone else, but with me this is the way things are. If you want me to continue working for you until you find someone else, fine. If not, I'm sure you know the number for the temp agency. They can send you someone else first thing tomorrow."

Their eyes were locked together.

Lucy could tell he was tempted to say that calling the temp agency was just what he would do, that he no longer needed her services. And she was surprised by how much she didn't want that to be the case. By how bad it made her feel to think he might walk out in the next few minutes and she'd never see him again.

But regardless of how she felt, she stood her ground. She wouldn't sacrifice time with Max to please Rand, to go on working with him, to go on seeing him.

Rand pushed off the archway then, finally coming into the room. He sat on the Bentley rocker that faced the overstuffed chair Lucy's fingertips were digging into the back of.

"You know damn well you're too good for me to give up before I have to," he conceded. Then he glanced around the room. "Are you hiding anything else I should know about?"

"You didn't need to know about this."

"I thought maybe you were rushing home to a boy-friend."

She wondered if that possibility had bothered him the way she'd been bothered by the evidence of the women in his life, but the only thing she gave him in response was a raised eyebrow.

It made him smile. Just slightly. A secret, satisfied sort of smile that left her thinking he enjoyed the fact that she was still keeping him guessing.

But he didn't pursue it. Instead he let the subject slide and said, "Now that I do know about Max—even if I don't know anything else about your life," he added facetiously, "what if when I need you to work later than five we do it here?"

"Here?" she repeated dimly.

"It wouldn't be every night. But tonight, for instance, after being away from the office all day, I could have used you. As it is, we'll have to spend tomorrow morning doing the finish-up work for to-day, which will give us a late start on tomorrow's work. But I don't live far from here. I'd be willing to continue things out of the office just to get them done."

Again she heard some sort of double entendre in his words but she once more decided it was only in her mind.

"I like my evenings with Max," she said, trying

to push away the sense that more was going on here than business.

"You'd be with Max. And so would I, for that matter. Unless I'm mistaken he liked me well enough. Between the two of us we could make sure he's not neglected but still get some work done."

Lucy had no doubt her son would like that arrangement. Max hadn't talked about anything but Rand the whole time she'd been getting him ready for bed.

"There would have to be an understanding that when we're on my turf, Max comes first. You'd have to be patient with interruptions."

"Fair enough."

Lucy was amazed at the change in his mood. Gone, suddenly, was the anger she'd been bathed in all evening, replaced by a coolheaded negotiator. No wonder the man was good at his job. He could be an intimidator one minute and an arbitrator the next.

"So do we have a deal?" he asked amiably.

"I guess so. But there's one other thing you'd better know. I did not appreciate being sent to run your errands today. I'm not your personal maid, valet or social secretary. Find someone else to pick up your dry cleaning, do your banking and send flowers to your girlfriends."

It was his turn to raise an eyebrow at her. "Sadie always took care of everything."

"I'm not Sadie."

He sized her up again, clearly debating whether to push this issue.

But once more Lucy stood her ground, not wavering beneath his scrutiny.

Then he took a deep breath, sighed it out and said, "All right. You drive a hard bargain."

"I'm worth it."

That made him laugh again, as if he were genuinely enjoying this.

"So if everything is settled, do you want to do some work now, while you're here?" she offered.

He shook his head as if that were the last thing on his mind. "I didn't bring anything with me or I'd say yes. But we may need to work tomorrow night to make up."

Making up was what it seemed like they were doing now. From a lover's quarrel.

But of course that was crazy.

Rand glanced around again. "You're renting this place from Sadie?" he said then, making yet another quick change into interested guest.

"We have an arrangement, yes."

"And she owns the other two in this section of row houses, unless I'm mistaken, doesn't she?"

"Yes."

"Good investment."

"Yes," Lucy answered yet again, trying to regroup and not being as fast at it as he was.

Putting some effort into it, though, she said, "Would you like something to drink?"

"No thanks."

Lucy finally rounded the chair and sat down just as Rand said, "Where is Max's father?"

That tightened every muscle in her body again. "He's out of the picture," she said curtly.

Rand reared back as if she'd struck out at him. "Sore subject and you don't want to talk about it," he guessed.

"There's nothing to talk about. He's out of the picture," she repeated firmly.

"Max is quite a kid."

"Yes, he is."

"Have you had his IQ tested? I've never met another kid as sharp as he is."

She shook her head. "I know he's bright, but I just figured it would be dealt with when he gets into school."

"I can tell you've given him a lot of time and attention. It shows."

"I try to."

"That's why you want to get into only freelance work, isn't it? So you can be with him."

"That's the plan."

"What about when he goes to school all day? Will you go back into office work then?"

"No. I'll use the hours he's in school to work at home and try to finish before he gets out in the afternoons."

Rand's smile this time was sheepish. "Well, you can't blame a guy for trying," he said, apparently having been fishing for a way to get her permanently onboard.

Lucy couldn't help cracking a smile of her own finally. It was flattering that he was so pleased with the job she'd done for him but there was also a part of her that hoped there was more to it than that. A part of her that she tamped down on before it got out of hand by thinking: *Deidre, Bunny and Veronica...*

"We flustered poor Sadie tonight," he informed her then, finding it amusing. "It was the first time in all the years I've known her that I've seen that. I thought she was unflappable."

"She usually is."

"I take it you didn't let her know you'd kept me in the dark about Max?"

"I wasn't proud of it. He's not something I hide in the closet."

Rand pointed a long, accusing index finger at her, narrowed his eyes and said victoriously, "Hiding him in the closet—that means you were lying not omitting."

"Semantics," she countered, unwilling to concede the point.

It only made Rand laugh. "I know where Max gets his brains but I hope he's not as stubborn as you are."

"I beg your pardon," Lucy said, pretending to take offense but laughing along with him just the same.

What was left of the tension between them seemed diffused and for a moment they sat there looking at each other the way two equally matched contenders might.

But then Rand stood. "I better let you get some sleep. I'm working your tail off tomorrow."

"Will you be in the office or out all day again like today?" she asked as they both headed for the front door again. She hated that it was so important to her that he'd say he was going to be in the office. Hated that the day without him there today had seemed so empty.

"I have a few court appearances in the afternoon but we can work in the car on the way into town and through the morning. Then again tomorrow night— don't forget that," he said. But the way he said it sounded more like he was reminding her of a date and this time Lucy didn't think she was just imagining it. There was definitely a more personal tone in his voice.

"I hadn't forgotten," she answered him, hearing the same sort of note in her own tone, although it hadn't been intentional.

Rand reached for the door handle when they arrived in the entryway and turned it but he didn't open the door. Instead he stood there looking down at her for a moment with eyes so warm they heated her to the core.

"I hope you know I don't put up with this much from anyone else," he said, his voice teasing but intimate, too. An intimacy that was very intoxicating.

"I hope you know I don't put up with this much from anyone either," she answered the same way.

Again he smiled and chuckled just a little, as if she never said what he expected her to.

And tonight when thoughts of him kissing her sprang to life in her mind, Lucy couldn't believe they were *only* in her mind. Not when his eyelids dropped slightly to aim his gaze at her lips. Not when he actually leaned forward just a bit. Not when he reached out and took her arm in a strong hand that set off lightning bolts in her bloodstream...

But in the end he only gave her arm an affectionate, playful squeeze and said, "No more omissions, okay? Be straight with me."

Lucy only agreed with yet another raise of her chin.

Or maybe she raised her chin in response to the lingering idea that he might kiss her after all. In response to the lingering wish that he would.

But he didn't.

He merely said, "See you in the morning." Then he opened the door and left.

Lucy rested against the door after he'd closed it, telling herself it was a good thing he hadn't kissed her, that it would have been totally inappropriate.

But deep down she couldn't ignore the disappointment.

Four

When Rand's phone rang at seven the next morning he was already showered, shaved and dressed for the day. He was just putting papers in his briefcase and trying to concentrate on the work he had ahead of him.

Trying but not succeeding.

His thoughts were really on Lucy.

He always screened his calls and while he waited for the phone to ring four times and the message to play, he felt a tight clench in his stomach at the thought that Lucy might be his caller. That after the end of the last evening she'd realized he had almost kissed her and now that she'd thought about it, about how out of line that would have been, she would let him know she didn't think it was a good idea for her to continue working with him.

It would serve him right, he told himself. What the hell had been going through his mind? She was his *secretary*. And she was a single mother on top of it. He didn't mix business with pleasure. Ever. And he certainly didn't have time for the complications of a woman with a child.

It was just that there they'd both been, standing at her door after sharing a conversation that had left him feeling as if they'd been on a date. She'd looked so soft, so alluring, so fantastic. And he'd been so tempted....

But after the fourth ring and the message, it wasn't Lucy's voice that came through his answering machine.

It was the voice of his adopted sister, Emily Blair Colton.

Shock froze Rand for a split second before he lunged for the phone as if it were a lifeline. Which it might very well have been, since Emily had been kidnapped out of her house in late September.

"Emily?" Rand nearly shouted into the receiver. "Is that you?"

"Hi," the young woman said tentatively.

"Are you all right? Where are you?"

"I'm okay," she answered, sounding it. "I know everyone believes I was kidnapped but I wasn't."

That shocked Rand as much as hearing her voice had. "What do you mean? What's going on, Em?"

"Rand, somebody tried to kill me," she said as if

the information had been building and building inside her and just had to come out. "The night I left. A man was right there in my bedroom. I barely got away and when I did, well, I knew I'd only be safe away from the ranch. Away from that woman who claims to be your mother," Emily finished in a derisive tone.

"Oh, Emily," Rand sighed, beginning to relax.

He knew what his sister was referring to. Since the car accident she and their mother had been in when Emily was eleven, Emily had never stopped insisting that their mother was not the same person. Just after the accident she'd sworn there had been "two mommies" at the scene—a "bad mommy" and a "good mommy," that the "bad mommy" was who had come home with her afterward. It was a claim she'd never wavered from, a nightmare Rand knew she was still plagued by.

"Where are you, Em?" he asked patiently.

"I don't want to tell you. But I'm okay. I've been in contact with Liza—"

"Liza knows where you are and that you weren't kidnapped?"

Liza Colton was Rand's cousin and another child his parents had basically raised, having spent more time at his house than her own. She and Emily had always been close.

"I had to get hold of Liza right after it happened," Emily explained. "She believes that woman is an imposter just the way I do, and I was afraid that put her in the same kind of danger I was in. That that woman would want Liza dead, too, so there wouldn't be anyone left to question who she is. I had to warn her.''

"Is Liza okay?"

"Yeah. But she's been telling me to call you, and I finally decided she was right. She said if anyone would help us prove that woman isn't who she says she is it would be you.''

Emily's voice echoed with such confidence in him that Rand didn't have the heart to let her know he didn't believe the woman he knew as his mother was an imposter.

"Tell me where you are, Emily," he said then.

"I won't tell you exactly where I am but I will tell you what state I'm in if you promise you won't tell anyone else. I'm even worried that woman might have bugged your phone, figuring I'd call you sooner or later. And if she finds out exactly where I am, she could send that man to try to kill me again.''

Promising not to tell anyone where Emily was was tough. He knew his father was out of his mind with worry over her. Rand himself had spent more sleepless nights than he could count since her disappearance, imagining the worst.

But he also knew that if he didn't make the promise to Emily she was likely to hang up without going any further and be lost again. He didn't want that.

"I promise," he said, albeit reluctantly.

"I hitched a ride with a truck driver," she confessed. Then, before Rand could comment on the perils in that, she added, "I know, it was a dangerous, crazy thing to do. But I didn't have a choice. I had to get away. And I figured if I was in danger in my own house, how much more danger could I be in hitchhiking? Besides, the man who picked me up was nice. Wonderful, in fact. He gave me the lecture himself about not doing what I was doing. Then he said he was going to Wyoming. Wyoming, Rand. Where Dad grew up. It seemed like a sign that someone was watching over me."

Rand closed his eyes against the thoughts of how naive this reasoning was. But now wasn't the time to get into that.

"Just tell me you're all right," he reiterated.

"I am. I'm fine. But will you help us?"

"You mean help you and Liza prove there's an imposter mother at the ranch?"

"Yes. Will you do it?"

"I don't doubt that someone tried to hurt you, Em. But what makes you think it wasn't an attack by a random someone who broke into the house to kidnap you?"

"I just know, that's all, Rand. I *know*. And he wasn't there to kidnap me, he was there to *kill* me," she insisted. "*Me*. Because I know that woman isn't who she wants everyone to think she is."

"There was a ransom note."

"I don't care. I know this wasn't an attempted kidnapping. I know that that woman who has everyone thinking she's Mom is evil, Rand. Please believe me and help prove she isn't who she says she is."

Rand heard the desperation in Emily's voice and it wasn't something he could ignore, even if he couldn't buy into Emily's imposter theory. But how could he convince Emily unless he agreed to do what he could to check out his own mother?

Besides, if he did as Emily asked, he reasoned, he could prove to her that she was wrong. That their mother was their mother and that the "two mommies" Emily was so sure she'd seen at the accident had only been a part of the trauma of the accident itself. Something that had festered in her mind as time had passed. Something that now had such power she believed it was the reason behind other, totally unrelated things that happened to her.

"I'll do what I can," Rand finally told his sister.

"Oh, thank you!" Emily said on a gust of breath, her relief flooding through the wires of the phone. "I know if anybody can find the truth you can."

"In the meantime, why don't you come here, Em? Stay with me."

"I can't," Emily said without thinking about it. "Then you'd be in danger, too. Just the way Liza is."

He heard the fear—no, the terror—in Emily's tone and he backed down. "What about money, then? Do you need that?"

"I only need your help, Rand. That's all I need. For you to find the truth and stop what's going on."

"Will you at least give me a phone number where I can reach you?"

"No. I'm in a phone booth now. I'll give you some time to look into things and then I'll call you."

"I want a promise from you in return for my promise to do this," he said then. "I want you to agree that if I don't turn up anything suspicious you'll go home.''

There was silence on the other end of the line for a long time before Emily said, ''I know you'll turn up something because I know that woman isn't who she says she is.''

''Promise me, Em.''

''If you can prove without a shadow of a doubt that that woman is your real mother, then okay. I'll go home,'' Emily vowed but clearly without believing that was going to happen.

''You'll let me know if you need anything,'' Rand said then, an order not an offer. ''And, Em, I'll get on the first plane to Wyoming if you say the word. To be with you there or to take you home to Prosperino, or to bring you here. You know that.''

''I know. But there's enough of us in danger already. As it is, I'm putting you at risk just doing this. If your phone is tapped and she finds out you're going to help me expose her, she could send someone to hurt you, too.''

''You just think about yourself and be careful. Let me worry about me.''

''But you'll start looking into this right away?'' Emily said hopefully.

''As soon as I figure out where to start, yes. Believe me, I want you home and this whole thing over with as soon as possible.''

''Thank you,'' Emily said, reminding him of the little girl who had become part of his family so long ago. "I have to go. Someone is waiting to use this phone."

"Take care of yourself," he said, not wanting to end their connection, worrying that it might be their last.

But there was no stopping it.

Emily said, "You take care of yourself, too," and hung up.

"The brachiosaurus is like the dinosaur giraffe only way, way, wa-aay bigger. Forty whole feet tall with a long, lo-oong neck with a little bitty head that weighs eighty tons."

"The brachiosaurus's head weighs eighty tons?" Rand asked, winking conspiratorially at Lucy as she looked on.

It was nearly eight o'clock that night and, good to his word, Rand had been patient with her son's interruptions of the work they were trying to finish up for the day.

"No, his head doesn't weigh eighty tons," Max answered as if Rand was just being silly. "His *body* weighs eighty tons. But his head has huge nose holes—"

"Nostrils," Lucy supplied.

"—high up on his head to keep him from getting too hot."

"And when did he live?" Rand asked.

"At the end of the Jurassic time."

"The Jurassic period," Lucy amended.

"*Nostrils* at the end of the Jurassic *period,*" Max

repeated to let them know he'd made note of both of his mother's corrections.

"And that's it for tonight's dinosaur lecture," Lucy said before her son could get started again. "Time for bed."

Max put up his usual fuss but finally gave in with a warm good-night to Rand.

Rand ruffled up Max's hair and answered the good-night with one of his own, leaving the little boy beaming as if Rand had bestowed the medal of honor rather than a simple hair mussing.

"I'll be right back," Lucy told her boss, appreciating his kind treatment of her son, who was obviously even more enamored by the man than he'd been the previous evening.

Max was already in his pajamas, having been dispatched to put them on earlier, so when Lucy got him upstairs she oversaw him brushing his teeth, read him a quick story and tucked him in.

"Can Rand come back tomorrow night, too?" the little boy asked as she kissed his forehead.

"I don't know. That depends on whether we'll still have work to do."

"He could just come to play if you don't have work to do," Max suggested.

"Oh, I don't know about that," Lucy hedged, wishing the idea of having Rand over just to play didn't have an appeal for her, too. "You just think about going to sleep now."

"'Night," Max said, wiggling around in his bed

with one arm around his bear. "Bart says 'night, too."

"Good night, Bart," Lucy said to the teddy bear, kissing its forehead the way she had her son's. "And good night to you, Mr. Max. I love you. Sleep tight."

As always Max was nearly asleep by the time she got to the door and turned out his light. And, as always, Lucy paused a moment to look back at him and revel in the peaceful sight of the little boy dropping off into dreamland. Then she closed the door halfway and left him to it.

As she passed by the bathroom next to Max's room, though, she hesitated. She had an inordinate urge to take a moment to check the mirror.

She shouldn't, she knew. It wasn't as if she were going back downstairs to a date. She was going back downstairs to work.

But she was powerless to stop herself and before she was even finished mentally listing all the reasons she shouldn't do it, there she was in front of the bathroom mirror, taking stock.

Her hair was caught in back by a clip and lifted into a geyser of curls at her crown just as she'd combed it that morning. But the curls had wilted slightly so she picked at them with practiced fingers to fluff them up again.

Her cheeks were still rosy, although she had a suspicion that was due more to the company waiting for her in the dining room than to the blush she'd applied before dawn. But her lips were dry and she reached for the remedy.

Lipstick or lip balm?

Lip balm was all she needed. Plain and simple. But what she grabbed from the medicine cabinet was the lipstick.

Don't analyze it and read more into it than is actually there, she advised herself, trying to believe that the fact that Rand was an extremely appealing man didn't have anything to do with her choice. But deep down she knew better.

Once she'd used the lipstick she took a quick glance at what she was wearing. The navy blue slacks and matching sweater she'd put on when she'd arrived home at the end of the day were still holding up. Not that she would have changed clothes if they weren't. But it was good to see she hadn't spilled anything on herself at dinner.

Then, as if the lipstick wasn't bad enough, she caught sight of her favorite bottle of perfume on the vanity beside the sink.

Oh no, I couldn't, she thought.

But her hand reached for the bottle anyway.

This is crazy. Inappropriate. Dangerous...

And worse than that, what if Rand noticed she'd come back downstairs wearing fresh lipstick and perfume?

That thought stopped her cold and she replaced the bottle on the counter. No way would she do anything that made it seem as if she were trying to seduce him. Because she wasn't. Seduction was the last thing on her mind.

So get back downstairs, finish your work and get him out of here, she ordered herself.

Though she might not be thinking about seducing him, she wasn't thrilled with the thought of him leaving.

She didn't want to admit it but she'd been looking forward to tonight. To being in the more relaxed atmosphere with him again. To this moment when Max would be off to bed and she and Rand would be alone...

Oh no, she definitely didn't want to admit *that*.

But it was true nonetheless.

"Just cool it," she whispered to her reflection in the mirror.

And she meant it, too. It was one thing to be hungry for adult company and indulge in a little of that. But anything beyond that was off the course she'd set for herself. Too far off the course for her to venture.

Even if she had been tormented since the previous evening, wondering if Rand really had been on the verge of kissing her.

Those thoughts evaporated when Lucy returned to the dining room where she and Rand had papers spread out all over the oak pedestal table. Like several other times during the day and evening, she found him staring into space, apparently lost in thought.

So lost in thought he didn't even notice she was back.

For a moment she stood in the doorway watching him. He looked terrific dressed in a pair of khaki slacks and a plain cocoa-colored sport shirt. His hair was only slightly mussed from some roughhousing he'd done with Max but it was every bit as attractive as when it was combed perfectly. Maybe even slightly more attractive because it gave him such a casual, approachable look.

But still his clean-shaven face was lined with what appeared to be worry and she couldn't help wondering what had caused it. What had been causing that same expression all day whenever he was left alone for a few minutes.

Several times that day she'd caught him making mistakes. Not to mention that he'd asked her to do the same things two and three times—even after she'd already done them—without realizing he was repeating himself.

It just wasn't like him. Something was on his mind, she decided, something that was distracting him. Maybe it was time she tried to find out what it was.

"Don't tell me. You're completely preoccupied with curiosity about the love life of the brachiosaurus," she joked to let him know she was there and to bring him out of his reverie.

He smiled, focusing his attention on her, but it was a weak smile. "I'm not much good today, am I?"

It was nice that he could acknowledge it, that he wasn't the kind of person to blame someone else when he was having a bad day.

"Seems as if you have something on your mind is all," Lucy answered, taking the seat she'd occupied most of the evening only a few inches to his right.

"Family problems," he said.

It surprised Lucy that he'd even confide that much and she thought it was an indication of just how troubled he was. But she couldn't be sure where to go from there. Should she accept that and let the subject drop? Or should she offer him the opportunity to get it off his chest?

"We don't have to work anymore if you aren't up to it," she said, tiptoeing through the trenches. "What's left here I can take care of while you're in court tomorrow."

He glanced at the work in front of them and seemed to make a quick decision. "Great. You'll probably do better without me dragging on you anyway."

But did that mean he was leaving? Lucy felt a twinge of regret that she'd even planted the thought in his head.

"You don't have to go," she heard herself say before she'd thought about it. Then, trying to cover her tracks, she added, "There's still some of that pie you brought and if it would help to talk about what's on your mind, I've been told I'm a pretty fair listener."

She didn't know if she was being too transparent, or if Rand had so much on his mind that he wouldn't notice.

For a moment he seemed to consider the pros and cons of her offer, and while he was at it, she fretted over the possibility that he'd realized some of the more personal things that had been flashing through her mind about him, that he might recognize the raw hunger in her for his company.

Then suddenly he said, "I think I could use another

piece of pie. I'll straighten up this mess while you do that and meet you in the living room.''

He sounded so pleased by the prospect.

Lucy's heart took wing despite telling herself to keep things in perspective, that it was probably just the pie he was really interested in.

But she didn't waste any time. She got up and went into the kitchen, joining Rand in her living room only moments later.

He was sitting on the couch and she thought it might seem standoffish if she sat on the chair instead, so she handed him a dessert plate with a healthy-size slice of key lime pie and then took her own smaller piece with her to the other end of the sofa.

''Did something happen back home in California between when you left last night and this morning?'' she asked then, in keeping with her initial intention to listen to his problems so he wouldn't guess she had also been rooting around for an excuse to extend his visit.

''It's a long story,'' he warned.

''It's early yet and I don't have any other plans,'' she assured.

''I guess things really started in '92.''

''It must be a long story if starts that far back,'' Lucy said with a laugh, settling into the corner of the couch so she could see Rand as he talked and trying not to notice the way his big hands dwarfed the small plate and fork he held. Trying not to think about the power leashed in them. Trying not to wonder what they would feel like on her skin...

"You're sure you want to hear it all?" Rand asked.

"Positive," she said too effusively, kicking off her shoes and curling her legs underneath her to prove she was committed to however much time it took.

"Okay. Well, when my adopted sister, Emily, was eleven, she and my mother were in a car accident. There were some minor injuries but the trauma was what really caused problems."

Rand went on to tell her about Emily's claim to have seen two mommies at the scene, about her continuing insistence that the woman everyone knew as his mother was an imposter, and about Emily's disappearance in September, ending with the phone call he'd received that morning.

"Could she be right?" Lucy asked when he was finished. "About your mother, I mean. It seems strange to me that she's stayed so steadfast all these years. It makes me wonder if she has some basis to believe it."

"I'll admit that that accident marked a big change in my mother," Rand conceded. "Everyone has seen that over the years. In many ways she isn't the same person she was."

"How so?"

"Before the accident she was about the sweetest person you'd ever want to meet. Thoughtful, kind, caring, generous, selfless. But since...well, since the accident she just hasn't been like that anymore. She's... I'm not sure how to put this. She's more intense. Material things mean more to her. She thinks more about herself than she ever did before. So there was unquestionably a personality change—maybe from a head injury during the accident. Obviously Emily sees that just as we all do. Only in her mind, coupled with the illusion or double vision or whatever it was she suffered herself in the accident, she's concluded that there really were two different people and the bad mother replaced the good.''

"So you think your sister took just that personality change in your mother too literally?''

"That's what I think, yes. Not that I want to diminish how frightening the accident was for Emily. And I don't doubt that something happened to her in September either. I just doubt that my mother had anything to do with it. But one way or another now I'm actually going to have to look into Emily's claims somehow.''

"What did you have in mind?''

"I don't really know. Maybe if I could get some background information on my mother, on her family. She's never talked a lot about it. Maybe that would at least give me a place to start. I just don't know what Emily wants from me.''

"I could probably do some of that on the Internet,'' Lucy said, thinking out loud more than anything.

Rand paused with his fork in midair. "You could?''

"I'm good at research, remember? Not only legal research. I've had some experience doing background research into people, too. I have a cousin who was adopted—an open adoption so her adoptive parents knew who her birth parents were but had long since lost touch with them. For health reasons my cousin needed to know as much as she could about her history, so I did some exploring on the Internet and managed to locate the information she needed as well as her birth parents. I think I can look into your mother's past without too much trouble.''

''Would you be willing to do that for me?''

''I don't know why not. It would be fun. You'd be surprised at what interesting things you can find out.''

He laughed and sighed at once, as if she'd just taken a huge burden off his shoulders. ''A great secretary and an Internet sleuth all rolled into one. Are there any of my problems you can't solve?''

She didn't know about his problems but there were a few of her own she wasn't having much luck with. Like getting her eyes to stop wandering to his broad shoulders. Like getting her hands to stop craving the feel of biceps that seemed to fill his shirtsleeves to the brim. Like curing the urge to slide across the sofa and press herself up against the hard wall of man that was Rand Colton.

But she didn't say that. Instead she said, ''Actually, when you were talking about hating that you couldn't put your family's mind to rest about your sister I had an idea about that, too.''

''Great. I'm open to anything at this point.''

''We could write an anonymous note saying that she hadn't actually been kidnapped, that she was okay, that she'd be home soon. Then we could put the note in an envelope, address it, put that envelope into another one and send it to a friend of mine in

Colorado. I'll call her and tell her that when she gets it to just put the enclosed envelope in the mail. That way there won't be a D.C. postmark to link it to you and it won't be traceable to your foster sister, either."

Rand laughed wryly. "That's a pretty good idea."

"You'd probably have thought of it yourself before too long."

"I don't know," he said ruminatively, studying her as if he were seeing a whole new dimension.

Then he said, "You know, I feel like I've struck gold in you. I thought Sadie was a hard act to follow but you're going to be impossible."

For some reason that seemed to put their brainstorming on a different level for her, relegating it to work, and it took some of the wind out of her sails.

But she was quick to remind herself that that was what they were doing there tonight—working. Whether it was on legal briefs or solving Rand's family problems, she was still just his secretary.

"Feel better?" she asked as if she were doing no more than he'd hired her for.

"Better than I have in a long, long while," he assured her in a voice that had somehow changed. It was deeper, richer.

His eyes delved into hers and just as suddenly as she'd felt reminded that she was nothing more than his secretary a moment earlier, things between them seemed to turn more intimate.

Was she imagining it?

Maybe. Because just as she was wondering where it might go from there, where she wanted it to go from there, Rand set his plate on the coffee table and stood.

"I should get out of here so you can have a little time to yourself."

What could she say to that? No, I'd rather have the time with you? Of course not.

So she stood, too, telling herself it was for the best that he leave before those unwelcome urges of hers got any more out of hand.

In the foyer she took his coat from the closet, trying not to notice that it smelled like his aftershave. She resisted the inclination to help him on with it, to put her hands on those big shoulders and smooth them down his back. Instead she merely handed it to him.

"I'll send the car for you in the morning but I won't be going in with you," he said as he slipped the coat on without any knowledge whatsoever of what the sight of it did to her. "I have a conference call to London so I'm going in earlier to do that."

"I'll finish up tonight's work on the way in then," she said, hating that they were once again back to business even though she knew very well that was the way things should be.

Rand headed for the front door but once he got there he didn't reach for the handle. He turned to look at her again with those cobalt-blue eyes that gave off enough heat to warm her as thoroughly as an electric blanket.

"Tonight was above and beyond the call of duty. It helped me to vent the family problems. I haven't really talked to anyone about what's been going on and it was nice to have some objective input. Not to mention your suggestions and offers to help.''

"It was nothing," Lucy demurred. "I'm happy to do what I can."

Rand's eyes held hers, his handsome face angled down at her so the full impact of his masculine beauty was right there for her to see—sharply angular bones, straight nose, square brow and those sexy, sexy lips....

And then out of the blue he kissed her.

He just leaned forward and kissed her.

Only a brief peck that could have been out of gratitude as much as anything. A brief peck that was there and gone almost before she knew it. Definitely before she could enjoy it or savor it or return it.

Do it again! her mind screamed. *Do it again, only longer this time!*

But of course she didn't say that.

"Thanks," he murmured then, his voice even deeper, richer than before, almost raspy.

All Lucy could do was nod because she was so lost in the desire for a repeat of that kiss that she couldn't find words to speak.

"See you tomorrow," he added as he opened the door.

"Tomorrow," she barely managed as he walked out to the silver Jaguar two-seater he had parked at the curb in front of her house.

Then he was in the car and gone, and she was still standing with the door open, staring outside and yearning inside.

Had that kiss only been out of gratitude? she couldn't help asking herself.

It was probably better if it was. But oh, how she didn't want that to be the case.

A man walking his dog sauntered past just then, looking in at her, and it finally occurred to her to close the door, that standing there with it open wasn't going to bring Rand back.

If it could, she might stand there all night.

Because more than anything she wanted him back, wanted him to kiss her again.

How could she not when that spare, nothing-of-a-kiss had heated her blood to flash point?

Five

The phone was ringing when Lucy reached the office doors the next morning. She could hear it faintly through the heavy oak panels as she tried the handle, found it locked and dug the key out of her purse. It took several rings before she finally managed to unlock the doors and rush inside. She was surprised Rand hadn't answered it himself by then. He didn't ordinarily stand on ceremony when it came to that.

She knew he was there. Besides the fact that he'd told her he was going in early for an important call, Frank had let her know he'd dropped Rand off at the office just before returning to Georgetown for her. Plus the television in his office was on and she could hear a news report on the stock market.

"Rand Colton's office," she said into the receiver as soon as she picked it up.

A client was on the other end, wanting to make an appointment. Lucy accommodated him, then hung up and heard her name called from down the hall somewhere in a voice that sounded like Rand's but different. Strained. Tight. Tense.

She took off her coat, laid it across her chair for the moment and went to see where he was.

Not in his office, not in the conference room, not in the copy/coffee room.

"Rand?" she called as she headed for the library at the very end of the corridor.

Her only answer was a combination growl and groan.

She poked her head into the library but still didn't see him. "Rand?" she repeated.

"I'm down behind the table," he answered through what sounded like clenched teeth.

Lucy went around the oval table and found him lying flat on his back, stiff and so immobile he looked frozen.

"What are you doing?" she asked.

"I just thought I'd grab a little nap," he ground out facetiously, definitely through clenched teeth. "I lost my footing on the damn ladder and fell off. Wrenched the hell out of an old college football injury in my back. I can't move," he explained irately.

"Uh-oh," she said. "What do you want me to do? Do you have medication of some kind you can take or is there a way for me to help you up?"

"Don't touch me!" he said as if she'd made a move to when she hadn't. "Call 911. I'll need an ambulance to take me to the hospital. My orthopedist's number is in the computer directory. Call him and tell him to meet us at D.C. General."

"Will you be okay just lying there while I'm gone?"

"No choice. If the disk has slipped, I could do damage by moving. Just hurry the hell up," he grumbled, clearly miserable.

Lucy didn't waste any time. She rushed out of the library and back to her desk where she made the calls he'd ordered her to make. "Help's on the way," she called to Rand when she was finished.

"Pack up the laptop and my cell phone and bring them with us to the hospital," he called back. "You'll have to get somebody to sub for me in court this afternoon. Try Spencer or White. Tell them to ask for continuances."

Lucy was in the process of doing what she was told when the ambulance and emergency medical technicians arrived ten minutes later. Their assessment of Rand's injury and carefully relaying him to a stretcher were the only interruptions to his clipped instructions to Lucy. Instructions that continued in the ambulance all the way to the hospital.

The doctor Lucy had called on Rand's behalf met them in the emergency room and took over from there, leaving Lucy in the waiting room to work while Rand was sent to X ray.

That set the course for the entire day. In between

X rays that determined that the disk had only slipped slightly, consultations with doctors, and treatments by physical therapists to manipulate the disk back into place, Lucy was by Rand's side doing his bidding, making necessary phone calls to cancel his appointments and rearrange his schedule and basically taking care of everything that needed to be taken care of.

It was only late in the day, when he was finally pumped full of painkillers and muscle relaxants, that things slowed down.

"You got a variance on the Clift case and the continuances you wanted on the others," Lucy said, giving him the wrap-up. "The Murphy brief is finished and ready to be printed out, the Kellog and Stanislov motions are filed, all the subpoenas on the Harris suit are set to be delivered tomorrow, I've cleared your calendar for the next couple of days and the doctor says I can take you home as soon as the release papers are signed."

"You're taking me home with you?" Rand asked with a devilish twinkle in his eye.

"I'm taking you home to your house," Lucy qualified. "Is that all you got out of what I just said?"

"That and you're a whiz kid."

Lucy fought a laugh. He was so relaxed he was lying in the hospital bed with a silly, contented smile on his face.

"I'm a whiz kid and you're high as a kite," she said.

"No pain, though."

"That's one good thing."

"So you're going to take me to my house?"

"I thought I'd call Frank to bring the car and get you set up there, yes. Unless you'd rather I have someone else meet you at home for that. I can always take the Metro back to Georgetown."

"Someone else?" he repeated dimly.

"One of your women friends."

"Women friends? Do people really use that phrase?" he asked with a giddy chuckle. Then he said, "No women friends. Just you. But what about Max?"

That "just you" had come out in a curiously affectionate tone but Lucy wrote it off to the daze he was in. "I've already called Sadie. She'll keep him at her place until I get there. She sends her sympathies, by the way, and said you should have known better than to climb that library ladder."

"Needed a book. Couldn't wait for you," he explained. "Thought I was being careful."

Which was something Lucy knew she needed to be because he was so sweet and silly and appealing in this state that she was having even more trouble than usual not falling victim to his charms.

A male nurse came in with the release papers and Lucy left the room so the nurse could help Rand into his clothes again.

When she got outside the room she telephoned Frank, who was there with the car by the time the nurse pushed Rand out in a wheelchair.

Getting him into the car was no easy task but they

managed, and Rand promptly rested his head against the back of the seat and fell asleep for the ride home.

It left Lucy in a quandary.

There was more work she could have done but she didn't have any inclination to do it. Instead her gaze kept straying to Rand.

There was no doubt about it, he was a very appealing sight.

His hair was mussed and gave her a glimpse of the way he must have looked as a boy. He had long, thick eyelashes—something she hadn't noticed before—so long and thick they put most women's lashes to shame.

His beard had reappeared through the day and shadowed his sharp jaw, lending him a rough, rugged look that only accentuated just how much man he was. Even his ears were sexy, with lobes that brought nibbling to mind. Nibbling Lucy imagined herself doing as a prelude to kissing her way down the strong column of his neck, along the rise of his Adam's apple to the dip just below it where a few coarse hairs peeked from his open shirt collar....

"Here we are," Frank said through the small window in the partition that separated the front seat from the back.

Lucy jolted out of the fantasy she'd involuntarily slipped into, overcompensating by sitting up too straight.

Rand opened only one eye and smiled a quirky smile that made her think he might not have been sleeping at all and might have known that she'd been taking a close look at him.

"My place?" he asked with a note of lasciviousness to his voice.

"Your place," Lucy confirmed, sounding like a drill sergeant.

She got out of the car in a hurry, rounding it from the back at the same time the driver rounded it from the front, and meeting him at Rand's passenger door.

Frank opened it and when he did Rand tossed Lucy his keys. "I'm the eighth floor. Go ahead and let yourself in. Have a look around while Frank gets me out of this car and I have a chat with the doorman before I come up."

Without comment Lucy turned to the building they were parked in front of, taking it in for the first time. It was a stately old eight-story brownstone and granite structure. Twin cantilevers wrapped around both corners almost like turrets, and a pillared archway led to the courtyard entrance.

A uniformed doorman opened the glass doors as she approached, looking beyond her at Rand and asking no questions.

The lobby was paneled in cherry wood and looked more like the bar in an elite men's club than a mere lobby. Lucy didn't hesitate to cross to the brass elevator, taking it to the eighth floor where it opened to only a short hallway and one set of double doors. Apparently the entire eighth floor was Rand's.

The key worked on the lock and she opened both doors, leaving them that way as she went in. The apartment was minimalist. Modern, stark, simple, yet lavish. Either he had perfect taste or his decorator did.

There was a five-foot sculpture in the entryway—a black-and-gray abstract piece that swung at the slightest touch like a pendulum between matching slabs of black marble.

To the left was the living room where three black leather sofas and two leather-and-chrome chairs were positioned in a square around a coffee table that was a piece of glass atop two stone cubes with a huge dowel that reached from the center hole of one cube to the center hole of the other like an artist's rendition of a barbell.

The room was very formal; the walls were lined with abstract paintings and sculptures, along with a sleek, black wet bar in one corner.

Beyond the living room was an equally formal dining room, this space done in browns, tans, golds and animal prints. It looked like a post-safari gathering place with an enormous oval table and twelve high-backed chairs.

From there Lucy found the kitchen, a wide-open area of streamlined stainless steel appliances and white tile so pristine and bright it nearly hurt her eyes.

Since that seemed to be it for that side of the apartment she retraced her path to the entryway and explored the opposite half, where Rand's home office was the first room she encountered. Also stark and spare, also black, white, chrome and glass, it was fully equipped with two computers, a printer, a fax machine, a paper shredder, a multi-functional telephone, a copy machine and file cabinets.

The master bedroom was just past that and since Rand had yet to come upstairs she went in without knocking. The room was slightly cozier, complete with an enormous king-size bed that sat low to the ground on a black Persian rug. There were two bureaus and a wall-length tropical fish tank, along with two more leather chairs and a large entertainment center that faced the bed.

Rand arrived just as Lucy was turning down his bed so he could get right into it.

"I have an electric razor in the medicine cabinet in the bathroom. If you'd get it for me, please?" he said as he eased himself out of his coat. "I don't think I'm going to get farther than the bed for now."

Clearly the trip from the hospital had taken its toll and Lucy wondered why he hadn't had Frank come up to help him undress. She certainly hoped he didn't expect her to perform that service.

Then, as if reading her mind, he said, "I thought I could manage to get out of my own clothes so I sent Frank to pick up some food. I don't know about you but I'm starving. I hope you like Chinese. Then he'll wait downstairs to take you home when you're ready."

"Yes, I like Chinese food, but couldn't Frank join us? I hate to have him just waiting for me downstairs."

"I invited him but he's bringing food for himself

and the doorman, too. They have plans for a game of rummy.''

Lucy nodded and then said, ''The shaver,'' to let him know she hadn't forgotten.

She was only too happy for the chance to go into the bathroom she'd barely glimpsed through the open door because even just that glimpse was enough to let her know it was spectacular. And it was. It was a large gray and white marble cove with a skylight for a ceiling. A free-standing sink stood below stair-step shelves of the marble that formed the shower, wainscoted the walls and provided four steps up to the sunken bathtub that nestled amid three stained glass windows that were works of abstract art all to themselves.

The medicine cabinet was recessed into the wall above the sink and Lucy had no problem locating Rand's electric razor. When she returned to the bedroom with it she found him struggling to remove his shirt, his face a grimace of pain before he realized she was there to watch. Then his expression just turned to stone.

But it was too late for him to hide the agony he was in and Lucy couldn't pretend she hadn't seen it. She also couldn't stand by without offering aid.

So much for not helping him undress.

''Why don't you let me help you with that,'' she said, setting the razor on the black enamel table beside his bed.

''Thanks.''

Lucy went up behind him and slid the shirt free,

trying as she did not to feast on the sight of his broad, straight back once it was exposed to her. But it wasn't easy to overlook rippling muscles that narrowed to a compact waist, all encased in sleek, smooth skin. Especially when she had the inordinate urge to press her palms to the wide expanse and test the texture to see if it really was satin over steel the way it looked.

"Can I persuade you to apply that ointment the hospital sent home with me? There's no way I can do it myself," he said, obviously unaware of what the sight of his incredible back was doing to her.

"Why don't we do that just before I leave?" she said, worrying that if she actually did touch him at that moment she might embarrass herself. She could only hope she might have more stamina later.

"That's probably a better idea anyway," Rand conceded. "If it works the way it's supposed to and numbs things, maybe it'll help me get comfortable enough to sleep."

"Right," she agreed as if that was what she'd been thinking all along.

"I'll go wait for Frank," she announced then, retreating from the room without another glance at her boss and reminding herself that what she was feeling was totally inappropriate.

Closing his bedroom door behind her, Lucy took a deep breath and exhaled it with gusto in an attempt to clear her head. She was there to help and nothing more, she lectured silently, and she'd better not forget it.

With that in mind, she marched to the kitchen

where she searched the cupboards until she found a pitcher for water, glasses and a tray to carry it all on.

Frank arrived with the food just as she was headed back to the bedroom so by the time she got there she had everything in tow. She knocked on the door and waited for Rand's "Come in" before she opened it.

He had shaved and was sitting propped on pillows against the enameled black headboard. He'd changed into a pair of gray sweatpants and had on a silk bathrobe over them that covered most of his upper half. His eyes were closed as if he were sleeping again, although Lucy thought it was more likely against the pain the exertion had probably caused him.

But when he heard her enter, he opened his eyes and his supple mouth stretched into a warm, welcoming smile.

"Dinner's here," she announced. "And I brought water to keep by your bedside along with your pills so you won't have to get up to take them during the night."

"Is there anything you don't think of?" he asked as she set the tray on his ample nightstand and began to unload it.

"Plates," she said, only realizing at that moment that she hadn't brought any.

"Let's eat out of the cartons," he suggested as if he didn't want her to leave again to get them.

Lucy pulled one of the chairs to his bedside and settled there to eat once they'd explored each container and decided where to start.

"How are you feeling?" she asked then.

"Not as good as I did before we left the hospital but not bad. That is if I don't try to move much."

"Will you be okay alone here tonight?"

"I can ring for the doorman if I need help. That's why I wanted to talk to him." Rand smiled wickedly. "Unless you're offering to spend the night..."

"I wasn't. I'll make sure you're fed and settled but then I'm going home."

"Spoilsport."

"Mmm," she agreed.

"We'll have to work here until I can get around again," he informed her then.

"From the equipment I saw in the other room it doesn't look like that will be a problem."

"It shouldn't be. These computers link with the office so you can access anything."

"Okay. But you're supposed to rest, you know. Maybe you should just tell me what you need done and not work yourself."

"I'd go out of my mind."

Lucy didn't question that. She'd seen enough of his intensity and energy level to accept it as fact.

"How did you hurt yourself originally?" she asked as they traded cartons of food.

"A mean tackle my senior year. I spent three weeks in traction, barely managed not to have surgery. I'm still trying to avoid it if I can, but every now and then I do something dumb—like climbing on that ladder that's really not big enough to hold me—and I get myself into trouble."

Rand asked if there was any fried rice left and once

he had what he wanted, he said, "So tell me about yourself. I know you're from California but I don't know where in California."

"Sonoma Valley. I was born and raised there."

"Are your folks still there?"

"No. My mother passed away last year and my father deserted us when I was seven. I haven't seen or heard from him since."

"That must have been rough."

"Rough enough."

"Brothers or sisters?"

"No. Just me, luckily. My mom had more than she could handle with only one kid."

Rand smiled that quirky smile again. "Are you telling me you were a handful?"

"No," she answered as if affronted by the very idea. "Well, I was a little mischievous but I didn't get into any real trouble. It was just that my mother wasn't equipped to support herself, let alone a child. And when it came to raising me, it wasn't an easy thing to do when she was dealing with her own emotional problems."

"Emotional problems?" Rand repeated to urge her on.

"After my father left she would go into deep depressions. She'd go to bed and not get back up again for weeks at a time."

"Would somebody else come in to look after you?"

"There wasn't anyone else. Sadie was here and she

was all the family we had. And my mother didn't have any friends to speak of."

"What would you do?"

"Everything that needed to be done. The cleaning, the cooking, the laundry. And I'd try to cheer Mom up. I'd do puppet shows from the foot of the bed. Sing and dance for her, tell her stories."

His smile this time looked sweet and troubled. "Did it work?"

"No, not really," Lucy admitted. "But I kept at it and eventually when she'd get up again I'd hope maybe I had something to do with it."

"So you learned to take care of everything—yourself included—and to be very efficient," Rand concluded.

"Good skills to have," she confirmed. "I also learned to value my own child and not to ever put him in a position where he felt like he had to parent me or needed to be the caregiver."

"In other words you learned to be a better mom through your own mother's shortcomings."

"I think so. I also think it's important to look at the positives that come out of every negative experience. I could never get my mother to do that. My father's leaving and not paying child support was bad, but it could have given my mom and me a chance to get closer, to have a better relationship, if only she would have used that opportunity. Instead... Well, instead she distanced herself from me and the rest of the world by taking to her bed."

Lucy caught sight of the clock on Rand's night table. She hadn't realized it had gotten so late.

"And speaking of taking to bed, I should get out of here so you can rest."

"I'm resting," he pointed out. "In fact, I'm enjoying myself."

"Still, I should get home." She gathered up the remnants of their dinner to take to the kitchen and dispose of there.

As she did she started to think about returning to the bedroom to rub that ointment into Rand's back and that was all it took to make her mouth go dry. To make her pulse pick up speed and her palms itch with anticipation.

Apparently waiting for a later hour had not allowed her any more stamina.

But what else could she do?

She could hope he'd forgotten about it and leave without reminding him. But that was irresponsible and cowardly and she would end up feeling guilty.

Which meant she was just going to have to meet the challenge. The challenge of actually touching Rand Colton and not giving in to what it would do to her. Not giving in to what it would arouse in her.

Steeling herself, she returned to Rand's room.

He'd moved to the edge of the bed, his feet flat on the floor, and it occurred to her that he didn't like her seeing him move without his usual agility or being witness to his flinching in pain so he did it when she wasn't around to watch. She liked that he didn't seem to want to wallow in the sympathy or the kind of attention that would garner.

"The ointment is on the bureau," he said then, moving only his chin in the direction of the dresser nearest the door, obviously not having forgotten about it.

Lucy retrieved it and crossed to him. "Stay where you are. I'll kneel on the bed behind you so you don't have to get up."

"You're the boss," he said with a note of levity in his tone.

Lucy gingerly maneuvered herself onto the mattress, getting into position with infinite care so as not to jostle him any more than necessary.

"If you untie your robe, I'll do the rest," she said, hoping it didn't sound as suggestive to him as it had to her.

But it must have because she heard a barely audible chuckle rumble from his throat before he complied.

When he had, Lucy eased the robe off the way she had his shirt earlier.

Just mind your business, she told herself sternly, opening the ointment tube and squeezing a little onto her hand.

"This might be cold," she warned, hating that her voice sounded so breathy, so intimate.

"The bad disk is slightly below my shoulder blades," he informed her.

Oh and what shoulder blades they were!

Lucy tried not to notice as she rubbed her hands

together to disperse the ointment and then pressed them to his back.

Satin over steel. She'd been right about that. Warm, smooth satin over honed steel.

"Tell me if I hurt you," she said, fighting to keep her perspective, to focus on the medicinal aspects and nothing more.

"Don't worry about it. You have a soft touch," he assured her, sitting there straight and strong.

He gave no evidence of pain. In fact it was Lucy who felt mushy-kneed and light-headed and at a disadvantage because the warmth of his flesh seemed to seep through her palms and infuse her with exactly the feelings she'd been worried this would cause.

She was much too aware of every inch of that broad back, of every rise of muscle and sinew, of every ridge of tendon and bone. So aware that it was almost difficult for her to breathe. So aware that her heart was beating as hard as a jungle drum. So aware that her blood was a rushing river in her ears. So aware that her nipples were standing at attention and making themselves all too known.

She went on rubbing Rand's back even after any signs of the ointment had disappeared into his skin, drinking in the wide expanse with her hands until she realized she was long since finished doing anything therapeutic and had begun to merely indulge herself.

"Okay," she said after swallowing her own rapidly rising instincts to go on, to explore biceps that bulged massively in his arms, to allow her hands to glide over his shoulders to his pectorals, to even test the waistband of those sweatpants he wore...

"That should do it," she added somewhat belatedly, willfully yanking herself out of her wandering thoughts and desires.

"Thanks," Rand said.

Was she mistaken or did his voice sound deeper? Maybe it was from the pain of sitting up.

Lucy eased herself off the bed and went around to his night table, taking stock of his supplies when what she was really doing was working to regain some control. "You have all your pills and water to take them with. The phone is within reach if you need help. Can I get you anything else before I go?"

He didn't answer her right away. But she could feel his eyes on her as surely as if they would make a mark.

"No, I'll be fine," he said finally, in a voice that was unmistakably raspier.

Then all at once his hand was on her arm, as if to stop her from leaving.

"Thanks for all this, Lucy. For everything," he said.

"You're welcome," she answered, unable to keep from looking at his face any longer.

And when she did she got lost in eyes that reflected his intelligence, his strength, his power and something more. Something that maybe she'd inspired...

Then that hand at her arm rose to the back of her neck and he pulled her gently but purposefully toward him, in command despite his debilitation, bringing her mouth to his.

It seemed odd that he could be the one kissing her under the circumstances but that was how it was. And tonight's kiss was no mere peck, nor was there a question that it might have been nothing but an expression of appreciation or gratitude. Tonight's kiss was much, much more. It was a real kiss. A kiss between a man and a woman. A kiss he deepened with lips that parted and urged hers to part, too. A kiss so adept, so tender, so just plain sexy, that it nearly curled her toes. A kiss that went on long enough for her to savor it, to come close to losing herself in it before it ended.

And when it did Rand looked deeply into her eyes and said, "I think you're a remarkable woman."

"I'd better go," she told him in the midst of a struggle to regroup, to remember why she shouldn't be doing this when every ounce of her cried out to just do it again. And again. And again. To do even more...

Rand nodded but went right on holding her eyes with his, fingering the tendrils of hair that had come loose at her nape.

Then he slid his hand to her shoulder and down her arm in a slow caress that left her stomach aflutter, squeezing her hand when he reached it and only then letting her go.

"Frank is in the lobby," he said with a note in his voice that made her think he was reluctant to lose her but resigned to it.

"What time do you want me tomorrow?"

Unfortunate choice of words. She only realized it after she'd spoken them and when Rand smiled that wicked smile of his again.

"Don't make me an offer I can't refuse," he said. Then he let her off the hook. "How about nine? I don't know what kind of shape I'll be in or how long it will take me in the morning to get my act together. Go ahead and take my keys so you can let yourself in when you get here in case I can't get to the door."

"Nine," Lucy repeated. "I'll be here."

"Tell Max hey for me and that I'm sorry to have kept his mom away tonight."

"I will. I hope you can sleep."

"Me, too."

Lucy stayed a moment longer, even though they really had dragged out their goodbye as much as they could, all the while telling herself to get out of there while she was still able to, before she leaned over and kissed him and restarted something she shouldn't.

Then, as if Rand knew how tempted she was and wanted to save her from herself, he said, "Go on. Maybe you can still get home in time to read your son a bedtime story."

Lucy just nodded, finally succeeding at breaking that magnetic eye contact of his so she could leave.

But as she grabbed her coat, purse and Rand's keys from the living room and rode the elevator down to the lobby she couldn't help recalling the feel of his back beneath her hands, reliving that kiss...that glorious kiss and all it had brought to life inside her.

And she knew as the elevator doors opened again

on the ground floor that it was a good thing Rand's health had made anything else off-limits. If it hadn't, she was afraid to think where things might have gone from there.

Because she honestly didn't know if she'd have had the ability to stick to her convictions and resist.

Six

Lucy had told Rand's driver not to bother picking her up the next morning. Since Rand's apartment was only two miles from her own home, it was easier for her to drive herself. Besides, it gave her the chance to take Max to day care.

She was pleased to see that what Sadie had told her was true—her son had already made friends. The moment Max got out of the car two other little boys ran up to greet him and off they went as Lucy followed them into the building.

"I'll pick you up a little after five," she called to him but her only acknowledgment was a brief glance over his shoulder and a wave before Max disappeared into the day care's gym while Lucy signed him in and left.

The doorman at Rand's building seemed to recognize her and to be expecting her when she arrived there a few minutes before nine. He had the door open when she reached it and greeted her with a hearty "Good morning."

And then she got on the elevator and succumbed to the jitters she'd been fighting.

Try as she might, in the last thirteen hours since leaving Rand's apartment, she had not been able to justify that kiss they'd shared. The peck of the night before that had been so inconsequential that it had allowed her to convince herself to some degree that it had merely been a buss of gratitude. But last night...

Last night's kiss was a real kiss.

And she wasn't too sure how to act after it.

It shouldn't have happened—that she knew. She shouldn't have *let* it happen. And she certainly shouldn't have been reliving it again and again in her mind ever since, like a teenager savoring a dream come true.

It wasn't a dream come true, Lucy told herself. She didn't have dreams about suave, sophisticated men sweeping her off her feet. She was a realist. Her dreams were about raising a good, productive son who would accomplish great things in his life. About having a wide circle of genuine friends whom she could count on. About traveling a little with Max or Sadie or her friends.

And as for romance? Yes, she had dreams of romance. Later. After Max was on his own. She had dreams of finding a mature, intelligent, responsible, prudent man who had sown all his wild oats and was in the market for companionship. She had dreams of a calm, sensible romance that would be two people coming together through mutual interests and values, both of them at the same place in life, wanting the same things, living the same kind of lifestyle. Settled. Secure. Low-risk romance. That was what she envisioned for herself.

Nowhere in even her dream was she a harried single mother rushing headlong into the arms of a man like Rand Colton who had women to spare and no room in his life for a ready-made family.

Yet there she'd been last night, kissing him.

And now she didn't know what to do about it.

Should she tell him it had been a mistake? That she didn't want it to ever happen again? That if it did it would mean the end of their work relationship and she would never see him again?

Or was that too dramatic? Would he look at her as if she were out of her mind and say it was not the big deal she was making it, that she should just forget about it?

Except that it felt like a big deal. A very big deal that had left her feeling branded by the man. That had left her weak-kneed and wobbly and wanting more.

Wanting more...

Now *that* was a big deal.

On the other hand, she thought as the elevator reached the eighth floor, Rand *had* been under the influence of a lot of medication. That might have contributed to his kissing her in the first place. He might not have been in his right mind, not in command of his senses. He might not have meant a single thing by it, nor even remember it this morning.

She liked that possibility the best. If he didn't remember the kiss, she wouldn't be the one bringing it to mind.

And as payment for taking the easy way out she vowed that a kiss would never happen again. No matter how much she wanted it.

After all, she wanted lots of things she didn't indulge in. Like banana splits for breakfast or brownies for midnight snacks or five-hundred-dollar shoes.

Or like men who could mess up the order she'd finally gotten her life into, distance her from her son and hurt them both.

So no, she would not indulge in any more kisses with Rand Colton, and that was all there was to it.

She just hoped as she put the key in the lock that the entire night before was nothing but a blur to him.

As Lucy went in she called, "It's me."

She half expected there to be no answer or to hear a weak hello from the bedroom. But instead Rand's deep voice called back a strong, "I'm in the kitchen."

Lucy took off her coat and set her purse with it on the art-deco wrought-iron hall tree in the corner of the entryway. Then she smoothed the red turtleneck sweater she had on over her black slacks.

She hadn't known exactly how to dress but had assumed that a workday spent in Rand's apartment didn't call for the business suits she wore to the office, so she'd opted for casual attire.

But when she reached the kitchen to join Rand she felt overdressed as he stood there in pajama bottoms and his bathrobe left open down the front.

Lucy's mouth went dry at that first glimpse of him, standing at the sink filling the coffeepot with water. Drier still when he finished and turned to face her.

He did it carefully, pivoting his whole body while keeping his torso and head ramrod straight, but it gave her a glimpse of what was beneath the bathrobe. A glimpse of a stomach that was a flat six-pack rising to a massively muscled chest spattered lightly with hair and shoulders so broad they were like a grand explosion of Old Faithful.

And it didn't help matters that his profoundly handsome face was shadowed in ruggedly masculine beard or that his dark hair was mussed as if from a night of lovemaking.

No secretary should be presented with such a sight and be expected to perform.

At least not to perform secretarial tasks.

Lucy knew instantly that keeping her vow was going to be the hardest thing she did all day because what she really wanted was to cross the space that separated them, slide her arms inside the flaps of his robe and start up where they'd left off the previous evening.

It took some doing not to succumb to that impulse, to hold her ground and say, "Good morning."

"Morning."

He gave her the once-over and there seemed to be approval—maybe even appreciation—in his expression as he did. Until he reached her upswept hair and then the slight smile on his provocative lips twitched just enough to make her think he didn't like the do.

She didn't know why that would be the case. It was the way she'd worn her hair every day since going to work for him, but even the faintest hint of displeasure from him made her want to reach up and unfasten the clip that held the spray of curls at her crown and shake her hair free.

But she steadfastly resisted that urge, too.

"How are you feeling?" she asked.

"I've been better. The pills make me too foggy so I'm only taking half the dose, just enough to blur the edges of the pain to get me by."

He didn't seem to want to discuss it further because then he launched into work-mode. "I've dictated some letters into the tape recorder that will need to be typed but I'd like for you to work up the anonymous note to my family about Emily so we can get that out. I thought if you wrote it there really wouldn't be any indication that it came from me. If you would, you can do that while I shower and then go on to the letters while I write the summation I have to get done. That'll also need to be proofread and typed. I doubt if we'll finish before noon but I thought we might devote the afternoon to the Internet search into my mother's background. I don't want Emily calling to check with me and not have something to tell her. Plus I'd like for you to be on the clock for that. I

GET 2

HOW TO GET YOUR
2 FREE BOOKS AND FREE GIFT!

1. Peel off the MIRA sticker on the front cover. Place it in the space provided at right. This automatically entitles you to receive two free books and an exciting mystery gift.

2. Send back this card and you'll get 2 "The Best of the Best™" novels. These books have a combined cover price of $11.00 or more in the U.S. and $13.00 or more in Canada, but they are yours to keep absolutely FREE!

3. There's no catch. You're under no obligation to buy anything. We charge nothing – ZERO – for your first shipment. And you don't have to make an minimum number of purchases – not even one!

4. We call this line "The Best of the Best" because each month you'll receive the best books by some of today's hottest authors. These authors show up time and time again on all the major bestseller lists and their books sell ou as soon as they hit the stores. You'll like the convenience of getting them delivered to your home at our special discount prices . . . and you'll love your *Heart to Heart* subscriber newsletter featuring author news, horoscopes, recipes, book reviews and much more!

5. We hope that after receiving your free books you'll want to remain a subscriber. But the choice is yours – to continue or cancel, anytime at all! So why not take us up on our invitation, with no risk of any kind. You'll be glad you did!

6. And remember...we'll send you a mystery gift ABSOLUTELY FREE just for giving "The Best of the Best" a try.

SPECIAL FREE GIFT!

We'll send you a fabulous surprise gift, absolutely FREE, simply for accepting our no-risk offer!

Visit us online at
www.mirabooks.com

BOOKS FREE!

Hurry!

Return this card promptly to GET 2 FREE BOOKS & A FREE GIFT!

The Best of the Best™

YES! Please send me the 2 FREE "The Best of the Best" novels and FREE gift for which I qualify. I understand that I am under no obligation to purchase anything further, as explained on the opposite page.

Affix peel-off MIRA sticker here

385 MDL C6PQ

(P-BB3-01)
185 MDL C6PP

don't expect it to be a freebie. We can put off the rest of today's work until tomorrow."

"Okay," Lucy agreed, grasping onto thoughts of work to help distract herself.

"I'm going to have to lie on the sofa in the office to do my part. Sitting is an exercise in agony."

"Can I fix you breakfast while you shower?" she offered.

"Thanks but I ate some toast to cushion the pain pills. Just pour us some coffee when it's done, if you would."

And with that he left to shower.

Lucy tried not to think about that as she went into his home office. Not to picture him dropping that bathrobe and those pajama bottoms. Not to think about the fact that he would be stark naked only a room away. Not to imagine thick-muscled thighs and well-honed calves, or a backside to die for, or a front side...

Oh, boy. This was not going to be an easy day at all.

She forced her mind off Rand and turned on one of his computers, laying out in her head the jobs of the hours ahead, picturing Max's cherubic face to remind herself of her own priorities.

It helped. By the time Rand returned, shaved, combed and dressed in sweatpants and a Harvard sweatshirt that still made him look all too good, Lucy had his coffee waiting on a TV tray in front of the couch and had already printed out the note for his family, informing them simply and succinctly that

Emily had not been kidnapped, that she was alive, well, not in danger and would return home as soon as she could.

"Great," Rand judged after reading it.

"I called my friend so she knows it's coming and what to do with it. I've also called FedEx to pick it up this morning. I didn't think you'd want to waste any time getting it to its destination."

"You read my mind," he assured her as he oh-so-carefully lowered himself onto the couch, his head and back elevated only enough to sip his coffee and write on the legal pad he set on his lap.

And with that they went to work as usual, spending the morning as Rand had instructed. Which was fine with Lucy. But it wasn't as much fun as the afternoon when she began to search into Meredith Colton's— nee Meredith Portman's—past.

"Some things are directly accessible," Lucy explained to Rand as they got started, sitting at the computer while he continued to lie on the sofa that ran the length of the wall beside it. "Things that are a matter of public record are basically there for the asking, but that doesn't mean I can just tap into the computer systems and bring them up myself. But I can e-mail a request for copies of things, which I did the night before last after you left. Last night when I got home I checked to see if any of my requests had been answered and when I found on your mother's birth record that she was a twin, I e-mailed for everything that was a matter of public record on her twin, too. I hope that wasn't out of line. I just thought that with your sister making claims to have seen two—"

"Twin?" Rand said, cutting her off. "What are you talking about?"

"Your mother was one of a double birth. You didn't know that?"

"No, I didn't know that. No one knew that. Are you sure?"

Lucy pulled up the e-mail and printed it out for him to see. Along with the birth information for Meredith Portman was documentation for a person named Patsy Portman, born on the same day, at the same hospital, to the same parents, five minutes later than the time of birth for Meredith.

"Why didn't you tell me about this right away?"

"I assumed you knew. Your mother didn't mention a thing like having a twin?"

"Never. Are you sure the twin didn't die shortly after birth? Or wasn't given up for adoption or something? Maybe my mother doesn't even know."

"I asked for everything that was a matter of public record on both Meredith and Patsy Portman. They both got driver's licenses when they were sixteen and the same address is listed on them. So your mother had to have known about her."

"What happened to her?"

Lucy wasn't crazy about being the one to inform him of this next part. She'd thought it was something he knew and had purposely not talked about because his family wasn't proud of it. "Patsy Portman has a criminal record, but I haven't delved into that yet. I thought you were aware of it and might not want me poking around in what was a skeleton in the closet, that that's why you hadn't mentioned the twin."

"A *criminal* record? No, I didn't know about that either. What did she do?"

Lucy felt very much the burden of being the bearer of bad news so she answered quietly, "She was convicted of murdering someone named Ellis Mayfair when she was eighteen."

"I need to know everything you can get on that."

"Old newspaper articles are the best but they're on microfiche. I might be able to persuade the library to fax us copies."

"Try," Rand said.

Lucy spent the next hour doing just that, luckily connecting with a helpful librarian in California who was willing to go to the trouble of looking for all the articles on the long-ago killing.

By the time the faxes began to come in, Rand had fallen asleep, and since the sound of the machine didn't wake him, Lucy read the articles herself.

It seemed that Patsy Portman had had a troubled youth wrought with mental instability, anxiety, bouts of depression and severe mood swings, all of which had been dealt with unsuccessfully by a caring mother who had tried to get her daughter help. Patsy had dropped out of high school and had been reported as a runaway several times.

Apparently in 1967 she'd become pregnant by Ellis Mayfair who was considerably older than she was and married.

Ellis Mayfair had wanted her to have an abortion but she had refused, hiding her pregnancy even from her family. She'd given birth to a baby girl in a motel room with only Mayfair in attendance, naming the child Jewel. But while Patsy had slept postpartum, Mayfair had taken the baby away.

When Patsy had awakened and asked for her baby, Mayfair had at first told her the baby had died. Patsy hadn't believed that and after pressing Mayfair was told that he'd sold the baby to a doctor for a secret private adoption.

Patsy had flown into a rage and attacked Mayfair, breaking a table lamp over his head and ultimately stabbing him in the chest with the scissors used to cut the umbilical cord, killing him.

Meredith had arrived at the scene shortly after the murder. But because of her presence before the police arrived, Patsy had tried to claim on the witness stand that Meredith had instead arrived during Patsy's fight with Mayfair and had killed him in defense of Patsy.

But Meredith had denied it and since there had been absolutely no evidence or witness testimony to support it, Patsy had been found guilty of second-degree murder and sentenced to twenty-five years in the state correctional facility for women in California.

Lucy glanced up from reading the faxes to see if Rand was still napping. He was so she went on to the follow-up article that had been done on the anniversary of the murder.

The anniversary article began with a jailhouse interview of Patsy, who was clearly obsessed with the loss of her child. The obsession seemed to the reporter to have pushed Patsy's delicate psyche over the edge. She was insanely angry with her sister for not having taken the fall for her. If only Meredith-the-honor-student and model citizen had said that she had killed Ellis Mayfair by accident while trying to defend Patsy, neither Patsy nor Meredith would have been put behind bars. But no, goody-goody Meredith wouldn't do that, Patsy had raved.

Patsy was also furious with their mother, Edna Portman, for not forcing Meredith to help. "But of course my mother wouldn't do that," Patsy was quoted as saying. "My dear mother wouldn't risk anything happening to her little pet, to the *good* daughter. But she couldn't care less if I molder away in a jail cell."

The reporter clearly doubted the credibility of Patsy's claims and upon investigation pieced together a timetable that put Meredith at the scene of Ellis Mayfair's murder only after the fact. The reporter had also learned that Mrs. Portman had done everything humanly possible in Patsy's defense, nearly to the point of bankrupting herself.

Additionally, the reporter had discovered that at Patsy's request of her family to find her lost baby, Jewel, Meredith and Edna—with almost no money left—had done their best to locate the child. But from reports by the prison guards, when Meredith and Edna had informed Patsy of their failure, Patsy had yet again flown into a rage, screaming profanities and telling them she never wanted to see them again.

After that Patsy had refused their repeated phone calls and visits, returned their letters unopened, and effectively cut herself off from them.

When questioned about this in a subsequent interview by the reporter, Patsy had admitted, "I washed my hands of both of them. I can't think of anything but my lost baby. My Jewel. I believe with all my heart that she's alive and I can only hope she's found a good home and knows somewhere in her heart that I'm just waiting for the day when I can find her myself."

Concluding the last article was an interview with Edna Portman in which she conveyed that while she was heartbroken over Patsy's tragedy, she was deeply concerned about what kind of impact this scandal was having on Meredith and what it would do to her future. In view of that she let the reporter know that she would no longer speak on the subject.

By the time the article had gone to press, Mrs. Portman and her daughter Meredith had moved to an unknown location, presumably in search of a fresh start away from Patsy altogether.

"And if I had to bet on it," Rand said when he'd awakened from his nap and read the faxes as Lucy had, "I'd bet that's why my grandmother and my mother moved to Sacramento, that it wasn't only for my mother to go to college. I'd also bet that my grandmother convinced my mother never to speak of the scandal again to escape the stigma and that's why no one knows anything about this."

"I wouldn't doubt it," Lucy agreed. "Especially

since it seems as if your mother and grandmother did all they could to help Patsy Portman and she made the decision to have nothing to do with them. They weren't abandoning her. They'd been shunned by her. But once that had happened and they needed to start over again, to make a new life for themselves, it defeated that purpose to tell people about it."

"But the question is, does all this have anything to do with what's happening in my family now?" Rand said.

"The articles mention more than once that Patsy and Meredith were identical twins. That, had Patsy not been wearing prison clothes, no one would have been able to tell them apart," Lucy pointed out.

"But after all the years that had passed between the time of that last article and when my mother and Emily had the car accident, is it logical to believe Patsy would have come back and done something as outrageous as hijack my mother's life?"

"It doesn't seem as if anything about Patsy was ever logical."

"Okay, granted. But even if she did impersonate— or *is* impersonating—my mother, how could she have pulled it off for so long? It seems so preposterous."

"What we see is usually what we believe. If Patsy caused the car accident Emily was involved in and switched places with your mother, chances are she looked too much like your mother to trigger any suspicions. But you said yourself that there was a difference in your mother after the accident. Maybe it wasn't a personality change at all. Maybe it was a *person* change, just the way Emily says it was.''

"I just can't imagine that. But if it's true, what did Patsy do with my mother?''

Lucy didn't want to respond to that because the most obvious answer was the worst. If Patsy Portman had gone to such lengths, for whatever reason might have gone through her deranged mind, to take over her sister's life, and if she had already committed one murder, wasn't it possible she'd committed murder again? That Meredith Portman Colton had met her death in that accident or just after it at the hands of her sister?

It seemed all too possible to Lucy but she didn't want to be the one to say it to Rand so she didn't say anything at all.

But he was so lost in thought that he didn't seem to notice. Instead after another moment of deep musing, he said, "You're right, Patsy tracking down my mother and causing that accident, then doing something with my mother in the process, would explain Emily's belief that she'd seen two mommies. But then it also means that my mother…isn't my mother at all.''

"And that Emily is right to fear for her life," Lucy said quietly. "She's the only witness to the switch.''

That troubled Rand even more. Lucy could see it in the deep beetling of his brow as he eased himself off the sofa and began to pace.

"So someone really could have been trying to kill Emily.''

"I know it's a horrible thought."

"As horrible as the thought that all this time Emily knew the truth and none of us believed her. As horrible as the thought that something happened to my mother and for years none of us has looked into it. Has looked *for* her."

There was a note of barely controlled alarm in his voice and Lucy knew how much this whole thing had rocked him. "Where will you go from here?" she asked.

Rand stopped pacing to look directly at her. "Good question. I didn't expect to find anything. I honestly thought that the attack on Emily was a random act of a burglar or something, that when we looked into things we'd come out with nothing but ordinary background information on my mother. I figured I could use it to calm Emily's fears when she called again and maybe convince her once and for all that she was mistaken about what she thought she saw at the scene of that accident and that everything else had just grown out of a young child's natural confusion—including her belief that someone was purposely trying to kill her. But now…"

He started pacing again. "Now what we've found sheds new light on what she's been saying. I think we've stumbled into serious territory that's going to require more than just surfing the Internet to find answers."

"I think you're right."

"But it has to be done carefully and by someone who actually knows what he's doing since we could have opened up a potentially dangerous can of worms.''

"True,'' Lucy agreed again, enjoying the sight of the wheels of his mind at work.

Once more he stopped pacing to stand at the window that faced the courtyard behind the building. "I have a foster cousin Austin McGrath. He used to be a cop but left the force in Portland to open his own detective agency. I think it's time to call him into this. Maybe he can find out where Patsy Portman is now. Or at least find a trail that could let us know if she's happily living in Cleveland and is absolutely not sitting in my father's house impersonating my mother.''

Lucy knew that was exactly what he was hoping but she had her doubts.

"Austin is good at what he does,'' Rand went on. "He knows the ropes. He'll be discreet. I'll feel better with this whole thing in his hands.''

"Do you want me to get him on the phone for you?''

Rand turned from the window to check the clock on the wall. It was a little after four.

"Thanks, but I'll get hold of him at home tonight. You've done more than enough for one day.''

If they weren't going to do legal work or pursue this family conundrum anymore, Lucy expected him to say she could leave early. But instead he said, "Close out the computer and let's take a little walk. I can use some fresh air.''

"Are you up to that?''

"If we don't go far. Walking is less painful than sitting. And I've been cooped up too long."

It was obvious that all the unsettling news she'd delivered today was really the problem, but she didn't say that. "A walk sounds nice."

She put on her coat while he took his from a closet in the entryway.

"Want help?" she offered.

"I think I can manage."

He managed all right. With difficulty but with the same stalwart determination that won him cases.

And while he was at it Lucy tried not to ogle him.

How could the simple task of putting on a bulky stadium jacket over a pair of sweats be sexy?

The answer was that on any other man it probably wouldn't have been. But on Rand there was an air of sensuality to it. So much so that by the time he'd put on the jacket Lucy *needed* a walk in the cool November air.

There was a park directly across the street and once they were outside that was where they headed. Only a few stubborn leaves still clung to the branches of generations-old elm, oak and maple trees, while the ground was blanketed in their gold and red brothers.

The air was crisp and redolent with the scent of wood burning in a fireplace somewhere. It was nearing dusk and the park was deserted except for the occasional dog-walker.

It occurred to Lucy that every workday should end with a leisurely stroll through a park to wind down.

"How did your parents meet?" she asked when

they had settled into a comfortable gait, still thinking about his family.

"Car trouble," Rand said with a chuckle that made it seem like a story he had fond memories of. "My father and my uncle Graham were on their way to Sacramento on a business trip and my mother's car was broken down on the side of the road."

"So your father rescued the damsel in distress and they fell in love at first sight?"

"My father fell in love at first sight, but my mother made a date with my uncle."

"Oh no!" Lucy laughed.

"Then my uncle stood her up."

"And your father stepped into the breach?"

"It was more like he saw his opportunity and took it."

"And once he had his chance with your mother, she couldn't resist him," Lucy guessed, thinking more about the son than the father.

"That's about the size of it, yes. What about your parents? How did they meet?"

"At a Christmas dance. My mother always said my father swept her off her feet, literally and figuratively." Again Lucy thought about Rand in that same regard.

"And maybe neither story had a happily-ever-after ending," Rand mused.

Lucy regretted having led him down this particular conversational path when it seemed clear that he needed to be distracted from it. So she said, "What's on tomorrow's agenda?"

"Today's work and tomorrow's, too," he answered wryly.

"Here again?"

Rand didn't answer immediately. But after a moment he said, "Here. I don't think I can make it to the office yet."

"Okay."

"I just realized this will be the first night this week that we haven't spent together," he said then, making it sound as if they'd done something much more intimate than working late or having dinner at her aunt's house.

"You're on your own, all right. Think you can handle it?"

"If I say no, will you stay?" he asked in a hopeful tone.

"No, I'd just give Frank a call. He said last night that if you needed a man Friday he was willing to do it."

"What *do* you have planned for tonight? A hot date?" he asked then, sounding more interested than she thought he should be.

"A really hot date," she confirmed.

"With anyone over three-and-a-half feet tall?"

"Height is no measure of the man. It's what's inside that counts."

"Is what's inside a whole lot of peanut butter and jelly?"

Lucy wondered if he was just teasing her with what sounded like a hint of proprietorship or if he had more than a passing interest in how she might be spending her off-hours. And the mischievous side of her was tempted to let him think she might actually have a hot date with someone other than her son just to see if it got a rise out of him. But she refrained.

"What's inside the man I'm keeping company with tonight is not only peanut butter and jelly, but ketchup, too."

Rand groaned. "Max eats ketchup on peanut butter and jelly?"

"He won't have it any other way." Lucy paused a moment but couldn't resist a little probing of her own, just in case. "What about you? Are you really spending the evening alone?"

"Why do you make that sound so implausible?"

Maybe because she'd seen his personal Rolodex and the names of women outnumbered the names of men six to one.

Lucy shrugged. "You just don't strike me as somebody who's good at being alone."

"I'm good at everything," he countered with a voice full of lascivious innuendo.

"Oh, excuse me," she joked.

"I thought about calling someone to come over," he said then. "But I'm having a little trouble in the female companionship area."

"Ha! Be careful who you're talking to. Remember I answer your phone. There are four women you owe calls to just since yesterday and I'm sure any one of them would rush right over at the snap of your fingers."

"No, the trouble isn't in finding company. The

trouble is that I've suddenly developed a lack of interest in any of them."

Was she imagining the underlying message in that statement?

"Since when?" she heard herself ask before she'd considered the wisdom and the fact that she was volleying his flirtation in a way she shouldn't have been.

"Since..." He pretended to count back the days since they'd met and then, instead, said, "Since you walked through my office door."

It was difficult to tell if he was joking because he made that sound as if he might be. As if he was just having fun with her.

So Lucy played along. "Well, don't worry about it. I have that effect on every man. It's a power I try to contain but sometimes I'm just not successful at it."

"You? Not successful at something? I don't believe it."

"My powers are a curse I've just had to learn to live with."

They'd made a loop through the park and now came out where they'd gone in, with Rand's building just across the street and Lucy's car parked in front of it.

"Now you're going to tell me that's it for today, aren't you?" he said, with a glance at her station wagon.

"It's about five."

"And you're going to leave me for another man," he said melodramatically.

"It's the appeal of the dinosaur trivia. You just can't compete."

"Don't rub it in."

That brought a flash of rubbing ointment into Rand's back the previous evening, just before she'd left. Just before he'd kissed her and she'd left.

It wasn't a thought that helped keep her equilibrium.

Lucy checked for oncoming traffic as Rand seemed more intent on looking at her and they headed across the street.

By the time they reached her car he was more serious again. "I really appreciate all you did today." Then he chuckled slightly. "I'm beginning to sound like a broken record."

"It's nice to be appreciated," she answered flippantly because she was still fighting the memory of rubbing his naked back and kissing him.

She unlocked her car door and opened it, stepping into the lee of it but not getting in.

Rand stood on the outside of the panel, carefully raising his arms to rest on the top of the window frame.

"Can I do something before you go?" he asked.

She could see the glint of devilishness in his blue eyes but she was too intrigued—and yes, maybe too hopeful that what he was going to do was kiss her again—to refuse him.

"What do you want to do?"

"This," he said, reaching around to unclip her hair so that it fell freely to her shoulders on a soft gust of autumn breeze. "I've been itching to do that since I met you. I just had to see what it looked like."

"And?" she said, hating herself for the need to know if he approved.

"And it's just as beautiful as I thought it would be," he answered simply, his voice quiet, his gaze caressing her hair in a way she could almost feel.

"I should go," she whispered, sensing that they had somehow once again stepped over that imaginary line from a work relationship to a personal one.

But Rand ignored the statement and let his eyes drift to hers, holding her gaze in a warm embrace for a moment before that same hand that had taken her hair down came to the back of her head again. Only this time it was to bring her closer so he could kiss her. Right there on the street.

But if anyone passed by or looked on, Lucy wasn't aware of it. She wasn't aware of anything but the feel of his mouth over hers, the wonderful return of what she'd been unconsciously craving since the moment his mouth abandoned hers the night before.

His lips parted and this time so did hers, without urging, and when his tongue traced the bare inner edge of them, they parted even more, inviting what she knew she shouldn't.

Rand accepted the invitation, sending his tongue to test the tips of her teeth, to greet her tongue before he enticed it to play, before he explored her mouth, before he deepened that kiss to such an extent that her car door between them seemed like a brick wall she wished would crumble away so she could be fully in his arms.

She wanted his hands on her body. Everywhere on her body, not just fingering her hair as if it were fine silk. She longed to shed coats and clothes, to feel his strong, powerful hands stroking her back, her arms, capturing her breasts in the warm hollow of his palm. She longed to feel his nimble fingers circling her nipples, squeezing them into even tighter knots than they already were.

And she'd do just as much touching of him as he did of her. Retracing those honed muscles of his back the way she had the night before, filling her own palms with his pectorals, trailing a path down his flat stomach, all the way down to the greatness she could only imagine.

One quick phone call, a little voice in the back of her mind said. *One quick phone call and Sadie will pick up Max. One quick phone call from upstairs. From inside his apartment. From beside his bed—*

"Rand? Is that you?"

It took a moment for the female voice to penetrate Lucy's thoughts. In fact it took a second, more insistent "Rand?"

But when it did, it was a bucket of cold water thrown on Lucy.

The kiss ended abruptly and both Rand and Lucy looked at the strikingly beautiful woman standing only a few feet away.

"Shelley," Rand said, his voice husky and almost

disoriented as he eased himself up straighter, releasing what hold he'd had on Lucy.

He regained his equanimity quicker than she did, introducing her to the tall blonde with the face Lucy had seen often on the covers of women's magazines and in makeup ads.

It took her slightly longer to come out of the haze that kiss had left her in, to actually say hello.

But the woman didn't seem to notice. In fact she barely seemed to notice Lucy at all, never taking her eyes off Rand to even look at her.

And Lucy felt awkward and out of place, and as if she'd been caught at something she should be ashamed of.

"I'd better get going," she announced, too loudly, she thought.

Then she got into her car without waiting for another word from Rand and closed the door.

She started the engine, seeing him only peripherally as he peered into the car and tried to say something to her. But she pretended she hadn't noticed and pulled away from the curb without so much as a wave goodbye.

What had she been thinking? she mentally shrieked at herself once she was on her way. Had she actually been thinking about not picking up Max? About going upstairs with Rand?

"Oh Lord," she lamented.

How could it be so easy to lose sight of everything? To forget herself? To forget everything she'd sworn to herself just that morning?

But she had. And if that other woman hadn't interrupted them?

Lucy didn't even want to think about where she might be at that very moment.

And yet she still said out loud, "You'd probably be where that other woman is."

That other woman...

Jealousy—hot and hard and hideous—struck Lucy and nearly knocked the wind out of her.

But other women were a reality in the world of Rand Colton, and she had better not lose sight of that fact, she reminded herself sternly.

So maybe Shelley Whatever-Her-Last-Name-Was showing up had been a good thing. Maybe it had been a protective reminder fate had sent.

Because not only had the other woman arrived in the nick of time, but she was also a glaring example of the difference between the life Lucy led and the life Rand led. A glaring example to remind Lucy that she was going home to a four-year-old whose visions of grandeur were a dinosaur movie and Vienna sausages cut up into his macaroni and cheese, while Rand was no doubt riding the elevator to his art-strewn apartment with a supermodel.

And as much as it might hurt for Lucy to admit to herself that she was only one among many women enamoured of Rand Colton, as much as it might hurt to admit that two such completely opposite lives could not be melded into one, it was nowhere near as much as it would hurt to have to recall those same things *after* she'd done what she'd been so tempted to do while he was kissing her.

"So thank you, Shelley Whozits, for saving me from myself," Lucy said with gusto as she pulled into the day care's parking lot to fetch Max.

But somehow she just didn't feel all that grateful.

Seven

———

Facing himself in the mirror the next morning wasn't the easiest thing Rand had ever done. In a way he was playing possum and it ate at him.

The spasms in his back had stopped and there was no reason he couldn't go into the office to work.

But had he called Lucy and told her that? Had he canceled their plans to work out of his apartment again?

No, he hadn't.

Because he'd liked having her in the more intimate setting of his home. Because as much as he'd enjoyed working with her every other day in the city, working with her at home had made him feel as if he had her all to himself. And he'd liked that too much to give it up today. He'd liked it so much it had made falling off the ladder and getting hurt seem worth it.

He rolled his eyes at his own reflection as he lathered his face for a shave. It was pretty bad when he was willing to play sick to get a woman to his apartment.

Not just any woman, though. Any other woman he knew would willingly come home with him—like Shelley the day before. He'd nearly had to be rude to keep her from coming upstairs.

But it wasn't any other woman he wanted in his apartment. It was only Lucy.

He was definitely having trouble in the female companionship arena the way he'd told her yesterday. More trouble than he'd realized if he was even willing to pretend his back was still on the blink to get Lucy up there.

But why? he asked himself.

All right, sure, Lucy was beautiful. Especially with her hair down—all those spirals of shiny mahogany. And of course there was that ivory complexion and those big blue eyes and those long legs and those full breasts. But he knew a dozen women equally as beautiful and not one of them could light his fire the way Lucy could.

It didn't help that she had brains to go along with the beauty. And a sense of humor. And warmth and compassion and understanding to spare.

But again, he knew several women with those same attributes.

They just weren't Lucy. Only Lucy could make his

heart go light with nothing but a laugh. Only Lucy made his skin sizzle every time she touched him, no matter how innocently. Only having Lucy around made even the biggest problems seem more manageable, the air seem more pungent, food taste more delicious, music sound more incredible, life seem more worth living...

"You've got it bad," he muttered to himself as he raised his chin so he could shave his neck.

He definitely had it bad. But for the wrong woman. And *that* was what he really needed to focus on.

Okay, she wouldn't be his secretary forever, so his rule about not mixing business with pleasure would be a moot point before long. But that didn't alter the fact that she was still a single mother.

And that was the real problem. That was what made beautiful, kind, compassionate Lucy Lowry off-limits to him.

Not that he didn't think Max was a great kid. He did. He got a big kick out of him.

But he was still a kid. A child who needed and deserved to be his mother's first priority and the priority of any man she brought into their lives. A child who didn't deserve to be shuffled into the deck of fourteen-hour workdays and business dinners and business trips and all-night research sessions and long, absorbing court preparations and the trials themselves. He didn't deserve to be reduced to the footnote of an adult's too-busy life.

Which was what Rand was convinced a relationship between himself and Lucy would do.

And that wasn't fair.

"So call Frank," Rand told his reflection. "Have him bring the car to take us into the city to work today and keep this thing in line."

But once he'd rinsed his face he didn't call for his car and driver. He couldn't make himself do it. Any more than he could make himself let Lucy go home an hour early the day before, the way he should have, the way he would have let any other secretary who had put in long hours all week and finished for the day.

But what had he done instead? He'd trumped up that take-a-walk ploy so he could have that last hour with her. So he could work up to kissing her again.

To kissing Max's mother...

But each time he'd kissed Lucy the last thing on his mind had been that she was anybody's mother. She'd just been Lucy. Lovely, lovely Lucy who smelled like spring breezes and felt like warm perfection and tasted like heaven...

"I'm here."

The lilting tones of her voice carried to him just then like an extension of his thoughts, of his daydream, and it took a moment for Rand to realize he wasn't just imagining it, that she had called to him from his front door as she'd let herself in.

"I'll be right out," he called back, shrugging into a chambray shirt he usually only wore when he was at the family ranch in California, tucking it into the jeans he also ordinarily saved for that same rustic environment.

He could still go out and tell her they were relocating to the office downtown, he told himself. Nothing was keeping him from putting on a suit, from telling her to go home and change—if she needed to—that he and Frank would pick her up there in half an hour. And then they'd be back in the more formal surroundings of his downtown office where maybe he'd have more luck keeping in mind that he should practice decorum rather than the subtle seduction he kept slipping into unwittingly around here.

But did he do that either?

No, he didn't. He left on the jeans and the chambray shirt and instead went in search of Lucy.

He found her in the kitchen and stopped short just inside the doorway to drink in the sight of her. She was dressed in jeans, too, and a cropped, rolled-neck sweater that let him see the way the jeans cupped her terrific rear end. She'd left her hair down—not completely free because she had a headband holding it away from her face, but down nevertheless in loose curls that danced against her shoulders and made him want to smooth them aside so he could press his lips to her neck.

And he just couldn't refuse himself at least having her alone there for this one more day, Max's mother or not Max's mother.

"How's your back?" she asked when she caught sight of him.

"Better. Much better. Almost as good as new," he admitted because he didn't want to out-and-out lie to her.

"We have a ton of work to do today. We should get started," he said more gruffly than he'd intended, overcompensating to cover the things that were going through his mind.

He saw her back straighten slightly, her chin raise a scant fraction of an inch and he knew he'd been too gruff. But all she said was a cool, "Of course. Yesterday's work and today's, too."

And then she left the kitchen and headed for the office portion of the apartment and Rand wanted to kick himself for starting their day off on that note.

But what could he do? he asked himself. He had to keep this strictly business, even if he was indulging himself in working at home for one more day.

Because no matter how much he indulged himself, it didn't change the facts.

And the facts were that Lucy Lowry was off-limits.

To Lucy there only seemed to be one explanation for the return of the aloof, arrogant Rand: that he'd spent the previous evening—maybe the whole night—with Shelley the supermodel, and as a result, now he wanted to distance himself from his temporary secretary and whatever it was that had been happening between them.

Well, that was fine. It was actually just what she needed. After all, she knew better than to have kissed him again yesterday. But she'd done it anyway.

She knew better than to have relived that kiss over and over again the whole night, taking it even further in her mind and working herself up into such a yearning, burning desire for him that she hadn't been able to sleep. But she'd done it anyway.

She knew better than to have gotten up this morning and primped and preened, put on her tightest jeans and a sweater that would play peek-a-boo with her midriff. She knew better than to have worn her hair down just to please—okay, and yes, to entice him and compete with the exquisite Shelley. But she'd done all of that anyway.

And most of all, she knew better than to foster any kind of flirtation with Rand or any other man when she'd made her decision to put that part of her life on hold until Max was grown. But knowing better hadn't stopped her from doing it anyway.

So if Rand could be aloof and distant and businesslike, so could she. Maybe that would finally put a stop to doing what she knew better than to do and was doing anyway.

Aloof, distant, businesslike—that was exactly how the day went. Rand never stepped out of boss-mode and Lucy never stepped out of secretary-mode. And not a single line was crossed all day long.

By four-forty-five Rand decreed them finished and Lucy closed down the computer with one eye on the clock, determined to leave at the stroke of five whether he suggested a walk in the park or not. She was anticipating a whole Rand-free weekend to get her wayward thoughts and desires under control, and nothing was going to stop that from beginning at five on the dot.

That was all that was on her mind when the doorman called up to announce a messenger.

She gave permission to send the messenger up, thinking that whatever was being delivered couldn't possibly pertain to work so late on a Friday afternoon.

But she'd underestimated someone, and when Rand opened the envelope he'd signed for and read the contents, he threw the documents on the desk and said, "Dirty son-of-a—"

"What is it?" Lucy asked before he could get the rest of his angry epithet out.

"The Turnenbill case."

"I haven't come across that this week."

"Believe me, that's a fluke. I've put more hours into that case than anything I'm billing for."

"You're doing it pro bono?"

"I do do that occasionally," he said defensively.

She hadn't doubted it, she just wished it weren't true because his handling cases for free was only one more aspect that made the man appealing. But rather than go into it she prompted, "The Turnenbill case?"

"Liz Turnenbill. Thirty-eight, mother of three small kids. She's crippled with arthritis and can't work. She was married to Tom Turnenbill, one of the heirs to an oil fortune. Six months ago he was killed in a car accident. Up until then they lived on dividends from a trust fund his family established for him and, surprisingly, didn't revoke when he married Liz."

"The Turnenbills didn't like Liz?"

"Bingo. She's not the debutante the family wanted

Tom to marry. They said they would never accept her and they didn't. They haven't ever even met their grandchildren.''

"Amazing."

"It gets worse. Tom had a will, leaving the income from the trust fund and his future inheritance to Liz and the kids. But when he died, his family revoked the trust. Liz and the kids were left penniless.''

"And no doubt her in-laws changed their own wills and she won't inherit what her late husband would have inherited, either.''

"Exactly."

"And since she can't work because of the arthritis—''

"They're destitute. In fact they were living in a house the grandmother had owned and the family even had Liz and the kids evicted. This—'' he nodded toward the papers that had just been delivered ''—is the latest response to our last go-round. I can't do anything to keep them from changing their wills so that Liz and the kids inherit what Tom would have. But I'm trying to get a ruling that bars them from revoking the trust, which is enough to leave Liz and the kids with enough to live comfortably, as well as to provide college educations.''

"Sounds like a worthy cause.''

"But the bottom line is that I need to do some fancy footwork in the form of research before the hearing they've pulled strings to schedule for first thing Monday morning or I may lose this case. If I do, Liz and those kids will never get what they right-fully deserve.''

''And you want me to work tonight,'' Lucy concluded.

Rand cracked a smile for the first time all day. ''I really didn't plan this. But if you stay and we do the research tonight I can use the weekend to prepare for the hearing.''

He held up a hand to stop words she hadn't even opened her mouth to say. ''I know. Max. So what if we call and ask Sadie to bring Max here? The four of us can have dinner. We'll order Max's favorite food no matter what it is. You can spend some time with him and then Sadie can take him home to bed while we finish working.''

''It just isn't possible to keep normal hours with you, is it? No wonder my aunt didn't want to come back to work even temporarily.''

He shrugged his shoulders and his eyebrows at once. ''Nothing I can do about this. It's part of the other side's strategy to try catching me off-guard. But I'm not going to let them win this. There's too much at stake for Liz and her kids.''

That struck a note with Lucy and she knew that even though another late night with Rand was inadvisable she was still going to end up doing it.

But before she fully agreed, she said, ''You want Max *here?* He'll be like a bull in a china shop. This place isn't exactly kid-proof.''

''I'm not worried about it. He can swing from the rafters if he wants to.''

Lucy gave Rand her most dubious look but finally said, "You'll have to call Sadie and ask her. I'm embarrassed to impose on her again."

"No problem. She loves me," he said with the debonair confidence of a man who knew his charms and the power they had. "While I do that, you can hit the books. Correction—you can hit the computer. See how much research you can do that way and if you can't find what we need we'll go into the office after Sadie and Max leave. I need whatever case law you can find on wills and trust funds, preferably something more recent than '62."

"Aye-aye, sir," she said with a salute, rebooting the computer and hoping the businesslike tone of the day could withstand the dark of night.

"Are you for-sure I can't ride it?" Max was referring to the sculpture in Rand's entryway that swung like a pendulum.

"I'm absolutely sure. You cannot ride it," Lucy answered for what seemed like the hundredth time since her son and Sadie had arrived. She herded the little boy back into the living room where Sadie and Rand were having after-dinner coffee.

When he got there Max stopped dead in his tracks in front of an abstract painting. "When I color like that, Miss Vanessa says to stop and start over and make it look like something. She says stuff like that's just a mess."

"Next time she tells you that, tell her she's inhibiting your creativity," Rand advised.

"She doesn't hit me," the little boy contradicted, either hearing wrong or giving *inhibiting* his own meaning because he didn't understand the word.

Rand and Sadie laughed.

"Inhibiting means she's keeping you from doing something," Lucy explained. "It isn't hitting."

But Max was on to a sculpture in the corner that looked like an abstract interpretation of a naked female torso.

"Shouldn't this lady have some clothes on?"

Apparently it hadn't been abstract enough.

"Would you like to see my fish, Max?" Rand said, obviously trying to distract him. "I also came across something I thought you might like to have. Come on in the bedroom and you can look at the fish while I dig out your surprise."

Max didn't have to be asked twice. "Where's the bedroom?" he demanded as he charged out of the living room and across the entryway again, making sure to give the pendulum sculpture a nudge to put it into motion as he passed it.

"I'm a nervous wreck having Max in a place like this," Lucy confessed to her aunt when Max and Rand were out of earshot.

"Rand doesn't seem too worried so you shouldn't be," Sadie responded, glancing in the direction they'd gone. Then she added, "Rand is good with Max."

"I know."

"He seems to genuinely like our boy."

"Luckily, since Max is crazy about him."

"So is Max's mom, isn't she?" Sadie asked slyly.

"Rand is a good man but that's all there is to it. I wouldn't be staying to work tonight except the case is one he's doing for a good cause. The Turnenbill case?"

"Mmm. He took that just before I left. For free," Sadie said as if Lucy might not know that. "He does a lot of that—donating his time, his expertise. You could do worse than a man like him, you know."

"I'm not *doing* anything but working. We're too different for any kind of personal relationship."

Sadie merely cast her a knowing look and took the coffee cups into the kitchen.

"Look-it, Mom!" Max said as he ran back into the room the way he'd run out of it. "Soldiers to fight the dinosaurs!"

Lucy looked into the shoebox full of plastic soldiers and toy tanks that her son was showing her.

"Rand says they were his when he was a kid, and since he doesn't play with them anymore, I can have them. If it's okay with you. Is it okay with you?"

Lucy looked to Rand, who had followed Max into the living room again. "You don't want to keep them for your own son, whenever you have one?"

"I might never have one," he answered as if it were the farthest thing from his mind and his plans.

Coming right after her brief exchange with Sadie, his words seemed to have a message in them. As if he were letting her know that although he might be good with Max he wasn't at all interested in parenting Max or any other child.

Take heed, Lucy, she told herself.

Sadie returned just then, carrying her coat and Max's too. "I think we ought to go home and let your mom and Rand get back to work."

"Na-aaww," Max moaned.

"It's almost your bedtime," Lucy pointed out. "I want you to get a good night's sleep and we'll have all day tomorrow together."

"With Rand?"

"No, not with Rand. Just you and me," she said, helping her son with his coat. "Did you say thank you for the soldiers?"

"Thank you for the soldiers," Max parroted.

"And thank you for dinner," Lucy coached.

"And thank you for dinner. And I like your fishes but I still think that naked lady needs some clothes," the little boy added with a giggle to let the adults know they hadn't fooled him.

"You're welcome for everything," Rand said with a laugh as they all headed for the door.

A round of good-nights and Lucy giving Max a kiss concluded the small dinner party and left Lucy and Rand alone again.

"What do you think?" Rand asked as soon as the door was closed behind Sadie and Max. "Are you getting what we need off the computer or should we take this to the office?"

Back to business without preamble, Lucy thought, feeling somewhat disheartened. But she went along with it, reminding herself it was for the best.

"I have a few things to check out through that law reference program you have. Let me see how far I can get on that. For now it looks promising and we may not need to leave here.''

"Great," he said with more enthusiasm than she understood.

In the end they didn't have to go to the office, but it took until nearly midnight for Lucy to accumulate the material Rand needed. And even then what she considered the coup de grace required some arguing on her part to get him to see it.

"I'm telling you, if you present it like this, it will be very effective," she insisted, giving him her interpretation of an obscure Supreme Court ruling in a 1971 case.

Rand shot out of his chair at the second computer to see the ruling for himself on her monitor when she was finished with her argument.

"Wow, your back must be a lot better," she commented, surprised to see him move with such speed and agility.

His smile was slightly sheepish. "Oh. Yeah, it is," he said as if he'd been caught at something.

But he didn't offer any more than that, instead reading the Supreme Court ruling over her shoulder.

"You could be right," he finally admitted after giving it some thought.

By then Lucy's mind was more occupied with the intoxicating scent of his aftershave than with legal precedent, and she had to force herself to concentrate.

"Actually I think you have a good point," he was saying. "If I use your angle, I think I can make it work for us. Print that out and let's celebrate."

"By calling it a day?" she said hopefully.

"I was thinking more along the lines of opening a bottle of wine."

It was a tempting idea. But with thoughts of leaving him to the supermodel the day before dancing through her head along with the full day and evening of his aloof attitude, she managed some restraint.

"You can't mix wine with the muscle relaxants for your back, and I have to drive home," she said.

"Okay, I'll open a bottle of grapefruit juice. But we've earned a reward. *You've* earned a reward," he said insistently, as if he wouldn't accept no for an answer.

Then he left her to do the printout, returning just as she'd closed down the computer for the second time that day.

He pointed with one glass to the sofa he'd spent the day before lying on and waited until Lucy was sitting there to hand her a glass. Then he joined her, angling so that he was facing her.

"To your hard work," he said, clinking his glass against hers.

"And to the work you still need to do all weekend," she countered.

"Yes, but you've made it much easier."

They sipped grapefruit juice and then Rand said, "Has anyone ever told you you have a sharp legal mind?"

"As a matter of fact, they have."

The expression on his handsome face let her know he hadn't expected that answer.

"I actually had a year of law school," she explained. "I wanted to be a lawyer from the time I was about thirteen and had my first debate in civics class."

"What happened to stop you?"

She'd avoided discussing this subject with him once before, when he'd asked about Max's father. But now—maybe because it was so late and she was tired and less on guard, or maybe because she'd come to know Rand better—she felt more inclined to tell him about it.

"Max is what happened," she said. "I got pregnant by one of my law professors."

"The father who's out of the picture," Rand said, repeating the very words she'd used to him before.

"Mmm. He was much older than I was, very attractive, brilliant. The dashing, serious academic who told me that I was not only beautiful but just as brilliant as he was, that I stimulated his mind *and* his body—"

"That isn't far-fetched, you know," Rand said in answer to her self-deprecating tone of voice.

"Far-fetched or not, I fell for it."

"You were young—"

"And naive and gullible and vulnerable and dumb."

"And you got pregnant," Rand contributed.

"And I got pregnant. I was so naive and gullible and dumb that I actually thought it might work out. That I'd tell him about the baby and he'd whisk me off to the nearest wedding chapel and we'd live happily-ever-after, Marshall the law professor, me the attorney, and our baby.''

"That didn't appeal to him?"

"Absolutely not. He was appalled by the pregnancy, let alone by any notion I had of us being together permanently. He said being married to one woman and having children were chains that would stifle him. That he was a scholar, not a husband and father. There was no place in his life, in the future he had mapped out for himself, for anything as stultifying, as repressive, as marriage and family. He wanted me to have an abortion,'' she ended that quietly.

"And you refused."

"I refused. He got nasty. He said he would never have anything to do with my bastard—that was what he called the baby. That he would deny being the father, that I would have to force paternity tests to prove it, that I'd never get a dime out of him in child support, even if it meant he had to leave the country to avoid it. Then he did more than threaten me, he told his colleagues that I had seduced him in an attempt to get grades I couldn't earn any other way and he managed to have my scholarship rescinded. It was through the school itself and had an ethics and morals clause attached. That left me without tuition, room or board on top of everything else. There was just no way I could go on with school. Plus I had doctors' bills and then a baby to support, so—''

"You had to give up your dreams."

"Dreams and romantic fantasies. But I gained Max.''

"Did you go through with establishing paternity and making the SOB pay child support?"

Lucy set her half-empty glass of grapefruit juice on the coffee table. "No, I didn't. After all that, I didn't want anything from Marshall. I didn't want anything to do with him. I didn't want to give him the opportunity to hurt me any more than he already had. Or worse still, the chance to hurt Max."

"What do you tell Max about his father when he asks?"

"That he lived a different sort of life than we do and so we couldn't be together. I know later on he'll want to know more than that, but for now he accepts it. I can see that he wonders why his father wouldn't choose him over anything else, but for the most part I don't believe it eats on him. I think he's pretty well-adjusted, pretty happy with just me."

"And you're very protective of him. Especially when it comes to letting men in."

Lucy laughed. "Of course. Protecting Max is my number-one job."

Rand set his glass on the coffee table beside hers and when he settled back again he stretched an arm along the sofa back.

Lucy had been aware of how little distance separated them but now it seemed like even less, and she wasn't sure if his arm running just behind her shoulders was the cause or if he'd actually moved closer.

Then he gave her one of those devilish smiles and said, "I could have used some of that protection yesterday."

"How so?" she asked, confused.

"You deserted me with Shelley Whitson. That was like throwing me to the wolves."

"Oh, sure. All men need to be protected from supermodels."

"Maybe not all men need to be protected from all supermodels, but I needed protection from Shelley. And what did you do? You abandoned me in my time of need. And me in a weakened condition, too. I'm lucky to be alive to talk about it."

Clearly he was trying to lighten the serious tone left by the recounting of her disastrous romantic past. But it was working because Lucy couldn't suppress a smile. Or the lightness that came to her heart at the thought that he hadn't been thrilled to be with the supermodel.

"How did you survive?" she asked, playing along.

"Only by my wits, since I wasn't up for any fancy footwork. But it was a close call. She was angling to get up here and when I tried to beg off by saying I'd hurt my back she offered to act as my private nurse."

"And you didn't let her?"

"No, I didn't let her," he said as if the very thought was repulsive. "There was only one person I wanted up here and she had just dived into her car and sped off as if she were escaping a mugger."

"So you were mad at me today," she concluded, more to herself than to him, thinking that explained the mood that had prevailed all day and into the evening.

"I wouldn't say I was mad. Perturbed, maybe. But

I can't seem to even stay perturbed with you for long." He was looking into her eyes and his voice had gone quiet and extremely deep. "I can't seem to stay any way with you that I know I should be staying."

She didn't know exactly what that meant, but when he took a strand of her hair between his fingers, she was hard-pressed to think much about it.

"You're doing something to me that I don't quite understand," he admitted then. "Something no other woman has ever done to me."

"I'm just sitting here," she pointed out, although her voice was unintentionally breathy.

"And even that's enough."

He wasn't making it easy for her to recall why she'd convinced herself not to enter into situations like this with him again.

"I'm trying to fight it," he confided. "But I'm getting nowhere."

That she understood. All too well. "I know," she nearly whispered. "I'm doing the same thing."

"Maybe we should stop fighting it."

"I'm afraid of where it might go if we do," she confessed quietly.

"We could take it just one step at a time. Carefully. Do a little exploring to see what's really going on here. Like research."

He said that with a half smile that made Lucy smile in return. "Research?" she repeated as if it were the worst line she'd ever heard.

He chuckled, a deep rumbling in his throat. Then

he kissed her, just a peck, and said, "What would you call it?"

"Playing with fire," she answered without having to think about it.

"But playing with fire leads inevitably to getting burned. Research just leads to knowledge and understanding."

"Is that what you want? Knowledge and understanding?"

He kissed her again, slightly longer this time, before he said, "Knowledge and understanding of what's going on between us, yes. Is that so bad?"

Bad? At that moment Lucy couldn't think of anything bad about being with him on that overstuffed leather couch with his arm resting across her shoulders now, his other hand toying with her hair, his mouth dipping down to kiss hers every few minutes.

But what she said was, "I don't know."

"I think we should find out."

"I don't know," she repeated just as his mouth covered hers again. Only this time the kiss wasn't merely playful. It wasn't merely a brief peck. It was a genuine kiss.

And of all the things Lucy didn't know, the one thing she *did* know was that she wanted that kiss. Oh, how she wanted that kiss! She wanted to feel his arms wrapped around her, his hand caressing her face, his lips parting over hers as hers parted, too.

All other thoughts faded into the background like twilight shadows and she lost herself in that kiss. Or maybe she gave herself over to it, because she was kissing him every bit as fervently as he was kissing her, meeting his tongue with hers when it came to call, sliding her arms around him so she could fill her hands with the hard muscles of his back that seemed no worse for wear now.

She definitely wasn't thinking about anything but that moment. About anything but the sensations alive in her. About anything but the yearnings that were rapidly awakening.

Yearnings to feel his hands on more of her body. Yearnings that brought her nipples to life, knotting them against his chest. Yearnings to be free of clothes, to feel flesh pressed to flesh, to learn the taste, the texture of every inch of him. To have him know her the same way...

They must have been of like minds because as Rand went on kissing her—hungry, openmouthed kisses—the hand that had cupped her face journeyed downward, barely brushing across her breast before coming to rest on her naked side where the cropped sweater had risen to expose her skin.

Shards of light erupted within her at that more intimate touch, surging through her with a whole new array of wants, of needs.

She sent the message with an arch of her back, with a deep inhalation that nudged her breasts more insistently into his pectorals.

Rand was nothing if not astute. He deepened their kiss at the same moment his hand coursed upward, finding the little nothing of a bra she'd worn today.

But even sheer lace was too much to have between

them and when he insinuated his hand beneath it to fully clasp her bare breast, Lucy couldn't help the moan of pleasure that escaped her throat.

An irresistible urge took hold of her and she pulled Rand's shirt from his waistband, plunging her own hands under the softened chambray to the hot silk of his honed back, his shoulders, his chest.

The snaps that closed his shirtfront popped under her vigor and she rid them both of the garment as if it were nothing but a hindrance. Which was exactly what her own clothes felt like—iron-plated armor that served no purpose but to keep her from the pure, uninhibited freedom she craved.

His hand at her breast was working miracles, raising her desires to a fevered pitch with talented fingers that traced and teased and pinched and rolled her nipples into a frenzy of longing.

His mouth left hers then and somehow she was lying back on the sofa as he eased her sweater and bra upward so he could see what he'd only felt before.

"Beautiful," he breathed as he did just what she'd been dying for him to do—he took her breast into his mouth, into that warm, moist, magical place where his teeth gently tugged and his tongue circled and flicked her nipple and things burst to life in Lucy that she hadn't felt in so, so long.

But something about the thought of just how long it had been since she'd been driven nearly insane with wanting reminded her of what they'd talked about earlier. It reminded her of times gone by, of how a moment like this could change so much. It reminded

her of another man, a man who might not have fraternized with supermodels but who had also lived a
life she didn't fit into.

Stop before you get hurt, a little voice in the back
of her mind shrieked at her, quelling just enough of
the emotions, of the desires, of the needs that were
rushing through her to let the warning register.

"Wait! Stop!" she heard herself say suddenly, as
if from a distance.

It didn't take more than that for Rand to do as she'd
asked, though. To stop and meet her eyes with his.

"Lucy?"

"This is more than one step at a time. We—we
aren't being careful," she said in a voice that sounded
as strained as she felt.

Rand laughed slightly, wryly, then kissed her once
more and sat up. "Fair enough."

Lucy sat up, too, adjusting her clothes and trying
not to look at the splendor of his naked torso because
her hands actually ached to be pressed to his steely
pectorals, to slide off his wide, straight shoulders to
his bountiful biceps.

"I guess I'm as bad as a hormonal teenage boy
with you," he said.

"Me, too. I mean I'm as bad as a hormonal teenage
girl." Lucy hated blundering through the words but
she was still reeling from the effects of what had just
happened between them, still struggling to find some
control.

"It's late," she said then. "I should get home."

Rand didn't respond immediately to that and she

thought he was working to regain control, too. In the end he must have accomplished it because he said, "I'd like to try to persuade you to stay but I won't. I'll behave myself and just walk you down to your car."

"No," she said, more quickly, more loudly, more frantically than she wanted to. But she knew if he walked her down to her car he'd kiss her again. And she also knew that one more kiss was all it would take to restart what had been so difficult to end. "It's better if I just go," she said to explain herself. "You're too tempting."

That made him laugh again, a sound Lucy liked much too much. So much she decided she'd better get to her feet, get some distance between them, or she still might succumb to the man's charms.

"Can I at least walk you to the door?" Rand asked as he stood, too.

"No. Just stay where you are," she commanded. "I can let myself out. Otherwise I might not get out at all."

In fact she knew that even if she stayed there devouring the sight of him any longer she might not have the wherewithal to go.

So she muttered a quick, "Good night," and headed for the entryway.

"Lucy?"

Rand had followed her as far as the doorway that connected his office with foyer and he stood leaning one shoulder against the wall there, his massively muscled arms crossed over his still-bare chest.

Lucy grabbed her coat off the hall tree and shrugged it on. "Don't say anything," she cautioned, feeling her will weakening even as she buttoned her coat.

"I just wanted to say thanks."

"Sure," she said, snatching her purse from the hall tree, too.

Then she escaped his apartment and the essence of him that seemed to be beckoning her back.

It was only as she drove home, working hard to cool off, that she wondered what he'd been thanking her for.

Had it been for the help on the Turnenbill case?

Or had it been for what they'd done on the couch?

Or maybe it had been for ending things before they'd gone too far.

She was still so churned up inside that she knew she was never going to be able to sleep tonight, and if Rand felt anything even close to what she was feeling, she doubted he'd be thanking her for that.

Eight

Joe Colton was sitting at the breakfast table the next morning when a FedEx envelope was delivered. Overnight mail deliveries were an almost everyday occurrence at Hacienda del Alegria, but somehow this one set him on edge. He wasn't currently doing business with anyone in Colorado.

Emily was his first thought. Something to do with Emily.

But then since her disappearance his daughter was always on his mind, and anything out of the ordinary raised hope that it had something to do with her.

"What's that?"

Joe was in the process of tearing open the envelope when Meredith came into the dining room.

"It's an envelope with a Colorado postmark. Do we know anyone in Colorado?"

Before his wife could answer, Joe had the envelope open and had pulled out a piece of plain white paper with only a few nondescript lines of black typeface on it.

"This says Emily is all right," he said excitedly as he read the missive.

"Is it from her?" Meredith demanded, not sounding as relieved as Joe was.

"No. I don't know. Maybe. There's no signature. It only says that Emily is fine. That she wasn't kidnapped. That she's safe, unharmed and healthy. That we shouldn't worry about her."

Meredith made a derisive sound. "That doesn't make sense."

Joe looked up from the paper he'd read and reread already. "Why doesn't it make sense?" he asked, wondering if he would ever become accustomed to the abrasive turn his wife's personality had taken in that long-ago car accident.

"It just doesn't make sense, that's all. She must have been kidnapped. Why would she leave? Why would there have been a ransom note?"

"Why would she or someone else send word letting us know she's all right if she *had* been kidnapped?" Joe countered. "It must be true."

"Well, I don't think it is. I think it's some kind of hoax."

"Let's let the FBI decide that. I'll get it to them and see what they make of it. But I don't see why anyone would bother with a hoax like this. It seems to me that someone is trying to reassure us. To put our minds to rest.''

''Believe what you like,'' Meredith said with her nose in the air. ''But I don't buy it.''

Meredith left the dining room then, as abruptly as she'd entered it, seeking privacy and a place to vent. The only place possible to do that was far away from the ranch, far away from the watchful eyes she always felt following her every move. When she'd driven far enough away, she stopped at a roadside pay phone and dialed the number she knew by heart.

''She's alive and well and maybe in Colorado,'' Meredith growled into the phone in answer to Silas Pike's hello.

''Mrs. Colton? Is that you?'' he said after a moment of apparently trying to put a name with the voice.

But the woman known as Meredith didn't bother to confirm who she was. Instead she said, ''I hired you to get rid of that twit Emily once and for all. I expect you to make good on that.''

''Just tell me where to find her and I'd be happy to.''

''I can't tell you where to find her, you imbecile. I only know that an anonymous note just arrived here from Colorado saying she's all right. But I don't want her to be all right. I want her disposed of. Do I make myself clear?''

''Colorado's a big place. How'm I supposed to find her with nothing more to go on than that?''

"That's your problem. Just do your job and do it right this time."

"I was feeling very disheartened and then last night I had a wonderful dream."

At the same moment that Joe Colton was headed to the FBI with the note about his adopted daughter, across the country in Mississippi, Louise Smith was meeting with Dr. Martha Wilkes, her therapist.

"Tell me about your dream," Dr. Wilkes urged.

"I was in a beautiful garden courtyard. There were bright flowers and tall trees—palm trees—like a tropical paradise. And there was a man, with dark hair. I couldn't see his face, so I don't know who he was. But he embraced me. Fleetingly, but it was so comforting. So comforting that when I woke up this morning my spirits were lifted and I felt as if I could go on, despite this being so difficult."

"Therapy, you mean?"

"Therapy, yes." That and knowing she was actually Patsy Portman. "And everything else, too. Knowing I actually killed a man, even though I can't remember it. That I'm a criminal. That I've been to prison."

"I can understand how troubling it is to learn about yourself, especially when you have no memory of any of it. But it's all in the past. Try to keep that in mind."

"Having a sister I wouldn't even know existed if we hadn't discovered that fact on the prison records isn't in the past."

"I've been thinking about that since we talked last time. I wonder if you should put some effort into finding your sister. Perhaps meeting her."

Louise hesitated. "I've thought about that," she finally admitted. "But I don't think I should do it yet."

"Why not?"

"I'm still trying to piece together who I am. But knowing I'm a murderess has a big impact. How do I know my sister wants contact with a murderess? Maybe I don't have the right to inflict that on her."

"But you've paid for your crime."

"Still. Until I can be clear about everything about myself, I don't want to face a sister I have no memory of. A sister I've apparently been estranged from since there were no records of her visiting me in jail, no letters from her in my belongings, since she hasn't tried to contact me in all the time since my release. Maybe when I get myself together and can present the kind of person she might want in a sister, maybe then I can find her."

"So denying yourself the sister you know is out there somewhere is your self-imposed penance?"

Louise thought about that before she said, "I guess in a way it is. Or maybe it's incentive to keep working to improve myself so I can be worthy of being in my sister's life again."

"This is your life, Lucy Lowry," Lucy said to herself as she stood in the open freezer door that evening.

"Saturday night and you're looking at a frozen dinner and a stack of old movies."

She'd taken Max to the home of one of his new friends for a sleepover and that meant she was on her own, a rare occasion. Despite the facetious tone of her voice, she wasn't unhappy about it. A few leisurely hours to herself, watching movies Max would never sit through, catering to herself for a change, was a nice break.

It was just that her thoughts kept wandering to Rand and what he might be up to on date night.

"A chicken pot pie it is," she said to distract her wayward mind, taking the package out of the freezer and closing the door resoundingly, as if that would put an end to Rand's occupation of her brain.

She would put the pot pie in the oven, she told herself, fill the tub with bubbles, condition her hair, give her face a mud mask, then curl up in front of the television with dinner and the pint of brownie fudge ice cream she'd bought as a treat. A night of pampering and indulgence—just what the doctor ordered after a long, hard workweek.

She was tearing open the package on the pot pie when the doorbell rang. She wasn't expecting anyone. After all, she hardly knew anyone in Washington. She doubted it was a door-to-door salesperson at seven o'clock on a Saturday night and she knew her aunt was having dinner with a man she'd met at a fundraiser the weekend before. So she was careful to peer through the peephole in her front door before opening it.

One peek was all it took to make her pulse pick up speed.

It was Rand. All dressed up, with a limousine parked at the curb behind him.

Lucy glanced down at her sweat suit, raised a hand to her pony-tailed hair, and considered not opening the door at all rather than face him looking the way she did.

But curiosity—and the instant rush of excitement that one glance at him sent through her—wouldn't allow vanity to rule.

So on the second ring she opened the door.

"I knew you were here," he said in greeting.

"I was in the kitchen," she answered as if that explained the tardiness that had required two rings.

The view through the peephole hadn't done him justice. He was dressed in an impeccably tailored suit cut too formally to be a work suit. It was a blue-tinged black and beneath it he wore a blindingly white silk shirt and a yellow tie that matched the pocket square that poked artfully from his breast pocket.

The clean, intoxicating scent of his aftershave wafted in to her, and unless she was mistaken, he'd had a haircut that had left his coffee-colored hair perfect and, at the same time, so natural looking.

"Are you going to invite me in or leave me standing on the stoop?" he asked then, with a crooked smile arching only one side of his oh-so-provocative mouth.

Caught ogling him, Lucy snapped to attention. "Of course. I'm sorry. I'm just surprised to see you."

"Surprise is the point," he whispered in her ear as he came in, striding past her into the entryway as if he owned the place. "My original plan was to whisk you and Max away for dinner to reward you both for the week I put you through. But I called Sadie first to find out if I had clear sailing, and she told me Max would be spending the night with a friend. So instead I'll whisk just you away."

Lucy had closed the door and was leaning against it, still fighting not to get lost in the jaw-dropping splendor of him.

"You're going to whisk me away?" she repeated, trying to grasp what he was talking about through the haze of his effect on her.

"First I'm going to give you about an hour to get dressed and then I'm going to take you to Aux Beaux Champs for dinner," he announced, his French pronunciation absolutely flawless.

Lucy hadn't been in town long enough to know about many restaurants or nightspots, but she had heard about the posh, four-diamond restaurant in the Four Seasons hotel. It was Georgetown's finest among a wealth of fine eateries.

"Aux Beaux Champs is quite a reward," she said, thinking that it was much more than that. It was a place for very special celebrations or very fancy dates.

"You put in quite a week. And after working all day long on the Turnenbill case and coming to the conclusion that you laid the groundwork for my likely winning it, you've earned a sizable reward. So what do you say?"

What did she say to a Saturday night in the best restaurant in town with the man who inspired things inside her that no one had ever inspired in the past?

Before she could say anything, Rand held up one hand to stop her. "I know. You're going to tell me you're my secretary and that it's inappropriate. But for just this one night let's put that on the shelf. Let's be two people who deserve a break, two people who enjoy each other's company, and go out for a little fun."

A little fun that would likely cost him what the average person paid in rent.

But how could she refuse? Especially when she wanted so much not to? Couldn't she do as he'd suggested and allow herself to let her hair down just this one night? Just this one night couldn't corrupt her whole life or the course she'd set it on, could it?

Okay, potentially it could.

But not if she were careful.

"Okay," she finally agreed.

"Okay," Rand repeated enthusiastically, as if he'd expected more of a fight. "Then point me to the remote control and I'll watch TV while you get ready."

"Would you like something to drink while you wait?"

"There's champagne chilling in the limo. I'll hold off until we can share it."

Even if he'd anticipated more of a fight, obviously he hadn't anticipated losing it.

Lucy didn't argue. She just showed him to the overstuffed chair in front of the television, handed him the remote control and hurried to the kitchen to put the pot pie back in the freezer.

Then she ran up the stairs to her bedroom, wondering if she was being totally stupid for doing this.

Okay, yes, maybe she was being totally stupid. But she didn't care. She was just too excited, too elated. Rand wasn't spending date night with another woman, he was spending it with her.

Just be careful, she reminded herself. *Be very careful....*

Lucy wasted no time taking her best little black dress out of the closet and then out of the dry-cleaning bag, carrying it with her into the bathroom. It wasn't wrinkled but there was a small crease on one shoulder that she knew the shower steam would relax.

From her hiding place in the back of the vanity where Max couldn't get into them, she broke out her favorite and most expensive gel and shampoo. But she didn't linger in the shower the way she would have liked, because she had too much more she wanted to do before her hour was up.

Once she was toweled off, powdered and perfumed, she blew-dry and scrunched her hair until it was a glistening riot of curls. Then she went on to makeup, using an artfully light touch with her usual blush and mascara, adding a soft pewter eye shadow and just a hint of liner, too.

She poked her late grandmother's pearl stud earrings into her lobes even though they could only be seen when her hair was brushed back. But they always made her feel dressed up and tonight that was what she wanted. It wouldn't do for her not to feel at her best when Rand looked the way he did.

At her best—that was what was still on her mind when she opted for the barely-there bra and panties she chose, along with the panty hose that were so sheer they made her legs look like they'd just come from a San Tropez vacation.

Then she donned her dress—a sleeveless, body-hugging length of matte jersey knit that traced every curve from the split-V neckline to the hem that ended two inches above her knees and left nothing to the imagination in between.

Last but not least, she slipped her feet into a pair of spike-heeled strappy pumps and carefully applied a plum-raisin colored lipstick too dark for daytime but just the right finishing touch for evening.

"Very nice," Rand said in genuine appreciation as he glanced over his shoulder when she descended the stairs fifty-five minutes later.

Off went the television and he stood, facing her so he could give her a second once-over from top to bottom and back again.

"Very, very nice," he repeated.

Lucy inclined her head to accept the compliment. "Didn't I hear something about champagne?"

"Champagne it is," he said, crossing to her to take her evening coat from her so he could help her on with it.

But once it was on, his hands lingered at her shoulders and he leaned in so close she thought he was going to kiss her ear. He merely took a deep whiff of her though and said, "You smell as fantastic as you look."

"So do you," she said since she'd been savoring the scent of his aftershave again.

He chuckled a deep, sexy chuckle. "I guess we should go out and knock 'em dead, then."

Lucy didn't agree with him immediately because as nice as the evening he had planned sounded, his touch, his nearness, his voice, everything about him sent a sudden flash-fire through her that almost made her want to stay home instead. With him. Alone...

Be careful, a voice in the back of her head cautioned.

"We'll have to go out because we can't knock 'em dead from here," she said when she could summon her voice.

Rand took his cue, releasing her to open the front door, holding it for her.

Frank was behind the wheel of the limousine and came out as they left the town house, rounding the car to open the rear door for them.

Lucy greeted the driver and exchanged pleasantries, then slid into the plush back seat with Rand following close behind.

"What happened to the Town Car?" Lucy asked when Frank had shut the door behind them, leaving them enclosed in the expansive gray interior complete with a tinted-glass window that separated them from Frank and an open bar where the champagne chilled in a crystal bucket and two glasses waited.

"The same service that provides the Town Car also

has limousines. It's my choice which I use and I thought tonight called for the limo.''

Rand poured the champagne, handing her one of the flutes as he settled back with his own.

''And you thought Max would do all right in this car and at Aux Beaux Champs?'' she asked with a small laugh at the notion.

''I had no doubt he would rise to the occasion.''

''Don't be too sure about that.''

''I figured there was a little gentleman lurking beneath the surface and we might bring it out in him tonight.''

''Well, one way or another it was a nice idea. But to be honest it's nicer to have an adult night for a change.''

Rand gave her a secret smile. ''I'm glad it worked out this way then. And I'll save all the dinosaur trivia I read up on on the way over for another time.''

Lucy laughed. ''You boned up on dinosaur trivia so you could make conversation with Max?''

Rand flipped open a compartment below the bar and produced a dinosaur book. ''I also thought if worst came to worst it would give Max something to look through. There are great pictures.''

If Rand was searching for a way to melt the last of her reserves, he'd found it because Lucy was touched by the trouble he'd gone to to relate to her son.

''You really are something,'' she said softly.

Rand didn't respond to that. He just put the book back in the compartment and closed it securely. ''But that's it for dinosaur talk. Unless you want me to woo you with the statistics of the Triceratops?''

"Are you wooing me?"

His smile this time was boyish. "Not so you're supposed to notice."

They'd arrived at the restaurant then and the valet opened their door before Frank had a chance. Rand got out then turned to offer her a hand, and Lucy accepted it without a thought, slipping her own into his much larger one as if it were something she'd been doing forever.

Once he had a hold of it, he didn't let it go.

It delighted Lucy more than she knew it should have. But it felt so good to have her hand in his. To walk into the elegant restaurant with such a man staking a claim to her in a way that all the room could see.

Rand was greeted by name and they were led without pause to the best table in the house where another bottle of champagne was already chilling. As the maître d' seated and welcomed them, the wine steward poured the bubbly elixir and an appetizer tray appeared as if by magic, laden with tiny pastries stuffed with crab and caviar.

And so their night truly began.

Over courses of soup, salad, succulent beef Wellington and artfully presented chocolate mousse cake for dessert, Rand kept up a conversation that might have bored someone else but was as much a feast for Lucy's mind as the food was a feast for her palate. He told her about his years in law school, about clerk-

ing for a Supreme Court judge, about the beginning
of his career, about his most interesting cases.

Once again Lucy held her own with him, asking
pertinent questions and even debating better ways he
might have argued two cases he lost.

Before she knew it, it was eleven o'clock and Rand
was suggesting dancing at a nightclub he knew of.

Lucy didn't hesitate to accept and off they went to
what looked like an old-time ballroom complete with
a full orchestra that played big band music from the
forties and fifties.

After the stimulation of their dinner talk it was nice
to take a more mellow turn, to be in Rand's arms, led
around the dance floor as adeptly, as gracefully, as he
did everything else.

Conversation slowed and they just let the music
waft around them, carrying them along until the wee
hours of the morning when the last song was played.

But somehow Lucy felt as if the evening shouldn't
be drawing to a close yet, as strange as that seemed
for someone who was usually asleep by midnight.

The truth was that she didn't want to say good-
night to Rand. Not yet. And so when the limo pulled
up in front of her town house again, she asked him
in for a nightcap.

He didn't hesitate to accept, countering with a suggestion that they stick with champagne and bringing
inside the bottle and glasses they'd started with.

Coming from a subtly lit restaurant and a dimly lit
nightclub, bright lamplight didn't seem called for so
once Lucy had shed her coat and folded Rand's suit

jacket over the banister, she led the way into the living room and turned on only one table lamp to cast an amber glow.

Rand poured them each more champagne but after handing her her glass he whisked her into his arms the way he had been all evening on the dance floor and began to sway with her as if there were still music playing.

"I think this was the perfect evening," he said.

"You make that sound as if it isn't something you do all the time and I don't believe that for a second," she countered with a laugh.

"That all depends on how you look at it."

"Oh? And how do you look at it?"

"I look at it as a rare occasion when I can share good food, good wine, good dancing *and* excellent conversation with a woman whose face I never seem to tire of looking at."

"Is that a line you use at the end of every Saturday night?" she joked.

He angled a mock frown down at her. "I do not use *lines*," he corrected. "And even if I did, what I just said was the absolute truth, so help me God."

"Well, now that you're sworn in..." Lucy said with a laugh.

"Go ahead. Ask me anything," he challenged.

"Are you drunk?"

He laughed that oh-so-masculine laugh that gave her goose bumps. "No, I am not drunk. I'm perfectly clearheaded." He set his champagne flute on the mantelpiece. "And rather than have you think for one minute that I'm not in full command of my senses, I will forego a single sip more.''

Lucy set her glass beside his. Not only because she'd had enough and didn't want to get drunk either, but also because what she really wanted was her hand free to place against his biceps as they danced.

"All right, you're not drunk. You're just smooth," she teased.

"Am I? I don't feel smooth when I'm with you."

"Why not?"

He laughed again. "Because you ruffle me up inside."

"Remember you're under oath," she reminded, her tone dubious.

"I remember," he assured. "The whole truth and nothing but the truth. The truth is that you ruffle me up inside."

"How do I do that?"

"Just by walking into a room. Or looking at me with those big blue eyes. Or giving me a run for my money intellectually. Or by smiling, or laughing or tilting your head the way you do when you're intent on something. You ruffle me up inside just by being you."

"What does that mean exactly? That I ruffle you up inside?"

"It means that my heart beats a timpani. That my blood runs faster in my veins. That I'm suddenly aware of every nerve, every sensation, every smell and taste and touch in ways I've never been aware of before. Sometimes I think you're spiking my coffee with love potion or something.''

''You've found me out,'' she said to make light of what was actually the same reaction she had to him.

His eyes met hers and they suddenly seemed somehow darker, deeper than normal. And when he spoke, his voice was more solemn, too. ''What are you doing to me, Lucy Lowry?''

''The same thing you're doing to me,'' she admitted in a near whisper.

''Do I ruffle up things inside you?'' he asked almost as quietly.

''Terribly.''

''I haven't been the same since the day I met you.''

''Neither have I.''

''Maybe we should do something about it,'' he said on a breath that heated her ear before he raised his head to look down at her again.

''Like what?''

He just smiled. A warm smile that said she could trust him. That opened him up to her in a way she'd never seen before, that let her know he was as vulnerable to her as she was to him.

He kissed her bare shoulder. Then the sensitive L of shoulder into neck. Then the side of her neck. Soft kisses that enticed, that entreated, that gave her the opportunity to tell him to stop before he reached her mouth.

But Lucy didn't tell him to stop. Instead she angled her head to one side to allow him free access, and lifted her chin when she knew her mouth was what he sought.

They were still swaying there in her living room as his lips took hers, swaying and kissing and holding each other.

And Lucy knew where this was going. She knew it as surely as if he'd drawn her a map. But tonight she didn't care about getting hurt or about incompatible lifestyles. Tonight Rand was hers and she was his and for that moment in time that was all that mattered. *He* was all that mattered. And that she wanted him. That she wanted to let this take her wherever it might. Just this once.

"I promised myself I'd be careful," she confided when one kiss ended and before another began.

"Does that mean I have to leave or that you'll just let me protect you?" he asked between nibbles of her earlobe.

Leave? Oh no, she didn't want him to leave and she told him so.

"Then trust me," he said in a voice that had grown gravelly, kissing her again.

Wisdom went out the window at that moment and nature took over.

Wide-open mouths were hungry, urgent, as tongues did a mating dance that replaced the swaying that had drawn to a close. Both of Rand's hands were in her hair, cradling her head against the onslaught of kisses she was returning with equal force.

Lucy's hands were busier, loosening his tie and taking a firm tug of both ends to hold him close while they kissed before she slid it from his collar and unfastened the top button of his shirt.

Without ending the play of mouths and tongues, she kicked off her shoes. Rand followed her lead, doing the same as his hands moved to her back so he could pull her closer.

She was thinking about taking him upstairs, about the fortuitousness of Max being gone for the night, when out of the blue something else occurred to her.

"Frank!" she said, breaking away from their kiss.

"You should never call out another man's name, Lucy. It's poor form," Rand deadpanned without missing a beat.

"He's outside waiting for you."

"Yes, he is," he agreed. He searched her eyes with his and then said, "Shall I send him home?"

He was giving her one more chance to opt out of what was happening between them. But Lucy didn't need to think about it again. She'd made her decision and now her body, her emotions, her needs, were in control.

"Yes," she answered in a breathy voice caused by Rand nuzzling her neck. "Send him home."

Rand let go of her only to take her hand in his and bring her with him to the phone on her corner desk. After punching in a number and waiting a moment he said, "That's it for tonight, Frank," and hung up.

There was something slightly embarrassing—and deliciously wicked—about taking that step. And now that they'd gone that far Lucy thought she was ready to take one more.

Without saying anything she led Rand up the stairs to her room.

Of course there really wasn't anything she needed to say. Or could say once they got there and Rand swung her back into his arms to recapture her mouth with his.

If there was hunger and urgency in those kisses before, it was nothing compared to this. All inhibitions, all hesitancy, all timidity seemed to vanish as wild abandon sprang to life.

That abandon made Lucy bold enough to yank at his shirttails to free them from his slacks. Bold enough to unbutton his shirt completely and then slide her hands inside of it to slip it off, to discover the glory of his bare skin.

And glorious it was. She let her palms travel over broad shoulders, down iron-hard biceps. She explored the steely expanse of his back, the rise and fall of muscle, the tautness of tendon.

That was when he started to lower the zipper down her spine and she was only too willing to have it done. Only too willing to let the little black dress fall around her ankles.

Their pace picked up even more then and off went what remained of Rand's clothes and then hers, until they were both unfettered by anything.

His hands came to her breasts, teasing, toying with them. Hands that felt new and familiar at once, lighting embers inside her that made a moan of pleasure echo in her throat.

Then as quickly as those hands had reached her

breasts they were gone again as Rand scooped her up into his arms and took her to the bed. He laid her down on it, lying beside her to capture her mouth with his once more, to cover one straining orb with one blissfully adept hand again in a kneading, thrilling caress.

He abandoned her mouth to leave a trail of soft kisses along the side of her neck, on the sharp ridge of her collarbones, down to that same burgeoning breast his hand had made ready for more.

Her back arched and there was no hiding the fact that he'd just lit fire to those embers inside her as his tongue circled the tight kernel of her nipple. As his teeth tugged. As he drew it farther into the warm wetness of his wonderful mouth.

While he was at that his hand went on traveling. Down the flatness of her belly. To her hip. To her thigh and back up again to stop at the juncture of her legs.

Lucy's shoulders rose completely off the mattress and her head fell back at that first touch, that first tender entry of stroking fingers.

But in this, too, she would not be outdone and so she let her own hand follow a path down his lean, hard body, grasping the hot, thick, sheathed length of him, savoring the power, the feel, the intimate knowledge of this man who had awakened so much in her.

He rose above her then, insinuating himself between her welcoming thighs, finding just the right spot and slowly pressing himself into her with agonizing care until she held him fully.

All on their own her hips reached up to him, accepting, relishing the union of his body with hers, eager for every sensation, every nuance, every flex of his muscles above her.

When he pulsed those first few pulses, Lucy gave herself over to him entirely, matching his pace, his rhythm, meeting him thrust for thrust on a magic carpet ride of the most perfect pleasure. Pleasure that grew and grew, that swelled within her like a beautiful balloon, filling her, completing her, lifting her higher and higher until every nerve, every muscle, was stretched to its limit. Until the balloon reached its holding power and burst into glittering glory that held her suspended for one timeless, extraordinary moment.

Only as she began to float back to earth by tiny increments did Rand tense above her, within her, melding them together in one final climax that was as magnificent to behold as it was to feel.

And she did behold it. She watched his bulging biceps and massive shoulders strain as they lifted his striking upper body skyward. She watched his handsome face freeze in a mask of pleasure that almost looked like pain. She watched him held in that moment of ecstasy as powerful wave after powerful wave washed over him, engulfed him, satiated him just as he had satiated her.

Then he, too, relaxed, muscle by muscle, settling atop Lucy in an exquisite weightiness, breathing heavily into her hair.

Minutes passed but she didn't have any idea how

many before he propped himself up with a forearm on either side of her head and kissed her again, a rich kiss that threatened to start everything all over again for her.

Except that the kiss didn't last long before he ended it to look down into her eyes, to study her face as if committing it to memory.

"Tell me you're okay," he said in a passion-raspy voice.

"I'm definitely okay. I'm better than okay."

That made him smile a satisfied smile. "Good. Me, too," he said on the gust of a sigh.

He rolled to his back then and pulled her to lie close beside him, to use his chest for a pillow.

"You're not like anyone else, Lucy," he said quietly and she could tell he was drifting off to sleep.

"Neither are you," she whispered back, unable to fight the lure of slumber herself, held there in the perfect cocoon of his arms.

But as drowsiness began to drug her, Lucy realized that the trouble with allowing herself this night was that she knew it would be over when she woke up.

And this one night had opened a floodgate of longing for more than just one night.

More of Rand and more of the things she knew she couldn't have...

Nine

Rand was awake before dawn the next morning as usual. What was different was that Lucy was beside him, that it felt like paradise, and that he had no desire to get up and charge into his day the way he did every other morning.

No, all his desires were aimed in another direction, but she was sleeping so soundly, so peacefully, he couldn't bring himself to disturb her.

What he could let himself do, though, was enjoy the sight she presented.

Sometime during the night she'd rolled to her other side, away from him. Now she was lying with her back to him, her head resting on his outstretched arm.

The top sheet and blanket had slipped down to offer him a peek at her smooth porcelain skin, perfect shoulders and the beginning dip in the small of her back, a spot he wanted badly to kiss right at that moment.

He resisted, knowing that would surely wake her, and instead pulled the covers up around her shoulders to keep her warm.

Her hair was a wild mass of curls all around her head, spilling over onto his biceps, and he reached his free hand to a mahogany coil of it, caressing it as if it were satin, committing the texture to memory, letting it coil from his knuckle to his fingertip.

He wasn't sure how long he was lost in that simple study of her hair. But it was long enough to make him wonder at himself.

It wasn't like him to be content with something like that. Content with lounging in bed. Content with watching someone else sleep. But he *was* content and he began to realize that the reason for it was that the someone else he was watching sleep was Lucy. And even when he told himself he should probably slip his arm out from under her, ease himself out of bed and go home, he couldn't make himself do it.

Sure he should. After all, it was Sunday. He usually called the ranch to talk to his family then. This Sunday he was particularly curious to learn if his father had received the anonymous note he and Lucy had sent about Emily. Curious to know the reaction his mother—if she really *was* his mother—had to the note.

But not even curiosity and family obligations could budge him out of that bed. Not when he was so happy just lying there, picturing what other Sunday mornings must be like there in Lucy's homey little town house.

He imagined that Max probably got up pretty early, too. That the little boy would be itching to wake Lucy, just the way Rand was—although for entirely different reasons. He pictured Max climbing into bed with his mom in hopes that he might jostle her out of sleep. Or maybe bringing his dinosaurs in and playing with them until he accidentally-on-purpose roused her.

She'd be patient with her son, Rand was certain of that. She'd probably grab him and hug him and laugh about him not letting her sleep in. Then she'd go downstairs and make him breakfast and the two of them would begin their day together.

But what would that same scenario be like if he was in it? Rand wondered, letting his mind wander a step further. What if he was in bed with Lucy when Max came in, holding her as she slept after a night of lovemaking like the one they'd just shared?

Maybe he and Max would nudge Lucy from slumber, teasing her, playfully ganging up on her until she opened those beautiful blue eyes of hers and bathed them both in that smile that was as sweet as warm honey. And maybe he and Max would go downstairs ahead of her and set the table, waiting for her to join them so that the *three* of them could begin their day.

Rand was astonished by how appealing that second fantasy was. All the more astonished because it wasn't something he would consider appropriate unless he and Lucy were married. And he wondered what had gotten into him to think such a thing.

But in truth he knew.

Lucy had gotten into him. Into his blood. Into his heart. Into his images of the future.

And that gave him pause.

Lucy and a future together? Was that really what he was thinking about?

It was, he realized.

She might not be a permanent fixture in his office, but that didn't mean she couldn't be a permanent fixture in his life.

Although he had to question whether or not it was a good idea.

Sure, it felt good to mentally place himself in Lucy's home, in Lucy's bed, in Lucy's and Max's Sunday mornings. But what about the rest of the time? he asked himself. What about Monday through Saturday when he was working abnormally long hours and preoccupied with cases and clients and trials? That was a whole different story.

That was the reason he'd avoided making any commitment to any woman, let alone to a woman with a child. The resentment and neglect he'd felt during his father's single term in the Senate when Joe had been away from home so much was something Rand had never allowed himself to forget. Something he'd sworn he would never inflict on anyone.

So what was he thinking now? That he would?

No. He wouldn't take on a wife and child the way things were. He still believed that was unfair.

But there was another possibility that occurred to him: he could make adjustments.

Wary of that notion, Rand mentally tiptoed around it.

Was he ready to make an adjustment like that?

He wasn't sure. But if he wasn't, if he didn't, what was the alternative?

Losing Lucy. And *that* wasn't easy to swallow. Especially not when lying there with her, wanting her again, wanting not to leave her, also made him realize that he didn't want to lose her.

It hadn't occurred to him until that moment just how much his life before Lucy had been lacking. How increasingly empty, shallow and unsatisfying it had seemed. That that was why he'd felt the way he had.

Yes, he'd been as busy, as harried as he had been since he'd set out to be a lawyer in the first place, but where early on that had made him feel fulfilled, somewhere along the way it had stopped accomplishing that.

Then Lucy had walked through his office door and he'd fallen victim to her beauty. To her special charm, her keen intelligence, her wit, her confidence. And he'd been rejuvenated. Not to mention turned on.

Now the thought of having her walk back out was unbearable.

So that left him with a choice, he thought. Either return to the way things were, to the ruthless determination to succeed without finding any joy in it when he did, or make a change. A big change. A change in favor of family.

Was it possible that after all these years of a high-powered, high-speed, workaholic lifestyle he had arrived at a point where family—having a family of his own—could suddenly be what he wanted? Could it be the key to his happiness?

That idea took some getting used to.

But once he had, he decided that it wasn't just *any* family that was the key to his happiness. It was the family that included Lucy and Max. The family in which Lucy would be his partner. Making the change was worth it for her.

Because the bottom line was that being with Lucy, making a life with Lucy and Max, had somehow become more important to him than work or money or acclaim or power. How else could he explain that when he weighed the life he'd been living and the discontent he'd been feeling against the contentment he felt at that moment, against the way he felt about Lucy, about Max, there wasn't a question that being with them won out?

Suddenly he knew that he was willing to do whatever it took to accomplish that.

Being a part of their lives would be better than any day's work, better than winning any high-profile case, better than anything he'd ever done before.

No wonder his father had been willing to give up a Senate seat to come home to his family, Rand thought then. As a child he'd been glad about it but had taken it for granted. As an adult he'd wondered how his father had done it, how he'd given up something he'd worked so hard to accomplish, something that meant so much to him.

But now he understood it. He understood what was genuinely of value, what *he* genuinely valued, and that was family. That was Lucy. That was Max.

The sun was barely up and he knew it was still too early to wake Lucy but he couldn't resist anymore. He couldn't just lie there having had the revelation of his life and not share it with her. He couldn't just lie there and not put into motion what he now knew was the answer to everything.

But what he could do was slip out of bed, go downstairs and make a pot of coffee, he told himself. Then at least he'd have a nice way to lure her out of her dreams.

And when he did, he had no doubt that she would fulfill all of his....

The smell of hot coffee was not something Lucy usually woke up to, and her first thought was that Max had done something he wasn't supposed to.

Her second thought was that maybe her aunt had come over.

It was only her third thought that recalled last night and the man she'd spent it with. She couldn't help the Cheshire-cat smile that stretched her lips even before she opened her eyes.

"Good morning," Rand said softly, beckoning her from sleep.

"It feels awfully early," she responded, still with her eyes closed.

"It is awfully early."

"Why aren't you asleep?" she asked much the way she might have inquired of Max.

"Couldn't sleep anymore," Rand answered with wholly adult mischief in his voice.

Lucy finally opened her eyes as Rand sat on the edge of the mattress. He was definitely a nice sight to wake up to. His hair was sleep-tousled, his face was shadowed with beard, he'd put on his slacks but left his incredible chest bare, and he looked so sexy it was hard for her to think about anything but pulling him back under the covers with her.

"How are you doing this morning?" he asked then.

Holding the sheet across her bare breasts, Lucy eased herself up against the headboard. "Any day that I have someone serve me coffee in bed I'm doing pretty well," she said, accepting the cup and taking a cautious sip. "How are you doing?" she countered, setting the cup on the nightstand to let the coffee cool.

"I'm doing stupendously." He nudged her over and sat beside her on top of the covers. "I've just had the revelation of a lifetime and I couldn't wait any longer to talk to you about it."

"The revelation of a lifetime, huh?" she said as if playing along with a joke. "I can't wait to hear it."

But maybe she should have waited. Forever, she thought as he laid out for her what he'd been thinking. Because the further he got into explaining that he thought he'd come to the point where he was ready for a family, for her and Max to be his family, the more panicky Lucy felt.

"No!" she said before he had finished.

"No what? I haven't asked you anything yet."

"No, don't go on. I don't want to hear this."

"Why not?"

What he'd said had agitated her so much she couldn't remain sitting still. Taking the sheet with her to wrap around her naked body, she scooted off the opposite side of the bed and put as much distance between them as she could manage.

"You don't know what you're saying," she insisted.

He was perfectly calm in the face of her storm, the preeminent attorney waiting to hear her argument. "I always know what I'm saying," he said reasonably.

"I know you're attracted to me as a novelty—"

"A novelty? You're putting yourself in a category with blow-up dolls?"

"I'm putting myself in the category I belong in— single mother. Those women you avoid, remember? Those women you don't even want as your secretary."

"Lucy—"

"No," she repeated, stopping him before he could go on because she didn't want to hear his reasoning. "You said yourself that you weren't sure you'd ever want to be a father because you can't give the kind of time and attention to a child that it deserves. You live a child-free life. A fast-paced, high-pressure life that has no place in it for kids. Look at your apartment, your clothes, your car—it's only a two-seater. Being around me and Max is nothing if not a novelty.

But that doesn't make it something you could do with any kind of longevity.''

''You think you know me better than I do?''

''I know that a man ensconced in his own life—a life that makes the world adapt to it rather than adapting to the world—is not a man who would ultimately be happy with the demands of a ready-made family. It's not a man who can take on a ready-made family without that family sacrificing everything to him. It's a man who would eventually want out, want back into his well-ordered life.''

''We're not talking about me, are we? Now we're talking about the law professor who left you pregnant and in the lurch rather than alter his agenda in the slightest.''

''We're talking about what I know from experience with Max's father and with you.''

''I've adapted to several changes while we've been working together.''

''No, you haven't. You've juggled and rearranged my life to get what you've needed out of the bargain. I'm not complaining, I agreed to it all. But only because it was temporary. I can't have a whole lifetime of that. I've only spent a fraction of the time I should have with Max since the moment I met you. That's not the kind of parent I want to be to him. It's not the kind of parent I *will* be to him. I've set our course and it's a course where Max comes first and I won't let anything or anyone distance me from him.''

''The last thing in the world I would want is to distance you from Max. I'm not talking about taking you away from him. I'm talking about adding me to the mix.''

"Why? So he can start to see you as his father, fall in love with you, depend on you and then watch you bolt back to your office, to your other life when you tire of the demands of a family and want out?''

"Let me see if I have all this straight. You think I'm some kind of male prima donna who, on nothing more than a whim, would swoop in, take you away from your son while insinuating myself into his affections, and then drop you both like a hot potato at the first sign of a scheduling conflict or a smear of peanut butter on the arm of the sofa?''

The cool, calm lawyer was showing signs of anger. He was on his feet now, too, facing off with her in a dauntingly arousing sight.

"My view of you is hardly that disparaging,'' she said, trying not to stare at the magnificence of his naked chest. "You're a good man, Rand. A great one. But you're a man who lives a life so completely different from mine that we might as well be on separate planets.''

"I'm not from another planet, Lucy. I grew up in a household full of kids and family. I know what it involves. I've avoided it myself *because* I know what it involves and I knew I couldn't have the kind of career I've had and a family, too. But I've had the career I wanted and it's falling short for me lately. It's not enough. Then you got dropped into my lap and I suddenly found myself feeling good again. Happy. Content. What I realized is that I've devoted enough time to my job and now I want to put it second to my private life. Now I want to make whatever changes need to be made to accomplish that.''

A part of her would have liked to believe that. To believe that he could actually pull it off. But she was afraid—no, terrified—that it was the same part of her that had believed Marshall would welcome the news of her pregnancy with Max, ask her to marry him and give her happily-ever-after.

But she'd learned that happily-ever-after was too good to be true, that she couldn't listen to that part of her that wanted to believe otherwise, no matter how much she might want to. That it only got her hurt and in trouble.

''No,'' she repeated once more.

''No what?'' he said again.

''I know you mean what you're saying right at this moment. I really do. But I can't trust it. I have Max to think about and I can't take the risk with him, with his feelings. He already likes you too much and—''

''I wouldn't hurt Max. I wouldn't hurt you,'' Rand said in a deep, quiet, sincere voice.

''I'm sure you wouldn't do it on purpose. But I truly believe that even if you put effort into cutting back on work, little by little it would creep in and take over the way it ended up taking over since I became your secretary. And Max would suffer. He'd suffer every time he expected you here and something came up at the office to keep you away. And he'd suffer more when you finally admit that cutting back isn't something you can actually do. That you thrive on the constant work, the pace, the world you've built for yourself, and that that really is where you belong.'' And she would suffer, too. Just the way she had when Marshall had turned his back on her.

"I'm not a boy, Lucy,'' Rand said very, very seriously. "I know myself. I know what I can and can't do. I know what I want. And what I want is not just a novelty or some passing fancy. It's you.''

"But I don't come alone. That's the problem.''

"I want Max, too.''

She shook her head, fighting the sting in her eyes. "It just wouldn't work out.''

"I'll make it work out.''

It was so tempting to trust in that. And if it had been her heart alone on the line she might have. She might have thrown caution to the wind the way she wanted to and just hoped that he honestly did know himself well enough to know he was capable of taking such an about-face with his life.

But she wasn't a woman alone. She was a woman with a child. A child she loved too dearly to ever put into any kind of risk at all.

"No,'' she said yet again, firmly and with finality.

"You won't even give us a chance?''

"No.'' She brushed the wetness from her cheeks with the back of one hand, wishing Rand was anywhere but there so she wouldn't have to fight to keep herself from running into his arms, from giving in to that naive, younger self who still yearned to believe everything he'd said and take the chance after all.

"I think you should go,'' she whispered, her voice

cracking traitorously and letting him know how close she was to breaking down completely.

"Lucy," he said, taking a step toward her.

"No," she said one final time, holding up a hand to stop him from coming any nearer. "Go," she added, but just barely because her throat was so full of tears she could hardly speak.

And then the phone rang. Of all the bad timing, the phone rang.

Lucy pressed a hand to her mouth in an attempt to gain some control, but before she did, Rand answered it.

She could tell by his clipped, curt questions that something was wrong. Very wrong. And another, different sort of panic took hold of her careening emotions and made the tears evaporate.

"What?" she demanded the moment the phone left Rand's ear.

"Max is hurt," he said, his own face blanched white. "He fell off the top bunk bed and hit his head. He's unconscious and on his way to the hospital in an ambulance right now."

Rand insisted on going with Lucy to the hospital, on driving her car because she was in no shape to be behind the wheel. They arrived at the emergency room twenty-five minutes later, both of them in clothes they'd thrown on without regard to anything but decency so they could get out in a hurry.

Max had already been taken for a CAT scan and before Lucy located the parents of Max's friend, one of the emergency room doctors came out to let her know what was happening.

Max had regained consciousness in the ambulance and exhibited no signs of concussion. But the CAT scan was for safety's sake. Of more concern was the fact that his left arm was badly broken and would need surgery to set it properly. Beyond that, he had a few bumps and bruises but he was fine and his prognosis was good.

Still, the mention of even the remote possibility that he might not come out of this with full use of his hand and the ominous tone of the surgery release forms did nothing to allay Lucy's panic. It took Rand's calming, logical reasoning to keep her from becoming hysterical.

When the doctor left, Rand guided her into the waiting room where Max's friend's parents were nearly as distraught as Lucy was. The couple apologized profusely for what was clearly more the boys' fault than theirs. Apparently the two had decided to play cliff diver off the top bunk bed and, being the guest, Max had gone first. In four-year-old reasoning, they'd been certain that the pillows they'd put on the floor would cushion their landing.

Lucy assured the other parents that she understood but she was in such an emotional state herself that it wasn't easy to deal with their remorse. She was grateful for the buffer Rand provided, and even more grateful when he convinced them to go home.

But that was only the beginning of the services Rand provided. Throughout the entire day he stayed by Lucy's side. She was all nerves and he was the calming force she relied on to get through. He brought her coffee. He repeatedly reminded her that her son was going to be all right, and he did it with such confidence she believed him until her own fear crept in again, and then he would reassure her all over again.

He got her to eat a small lunch while Max was being operated on by Washington's leading pediatric surgeon, a man Rand knew and had called in personally. Rand held her hand. He even managed to make her laugh a time or two. He called Sadie to let her know what had happened and when Sadie arrived at the hospital with a small bag of things for Lucy to use to clean up, comb her hair and stay the night with Max, Rand treated Sadie's worry as tenderly as he continued to treat Lucy's.

By late that evening Max was sleeping peacefully in a private room that Rand had arranged for. The little boy had come through the surgery with flying colors and had awakened long enough to prove he could move all five fingers without a problem before drifting off to sleep again.

When visiting hours ended, Sadie kissed the sleeping Max. Then Lucy, Sadie and Rand went out into the hall.

"Anything you need, darling, just call," Sadie told Lucy, kissing her, too. "Otherwise I'll see you in the morning when you get our boy home."

"I'll be fine," Lucy answered, accepting her aunt's

hug and letting Sadie know she finally did feel certain things really were going to be okay.

Then Sadie headed for the elevator, leaving Lucy and Rand alone.

"I'm taking your car back to your place," he explained in a hushed tone so as not to disturb Max through the open door. "I'll have Frank pick me up there and he'll be back here first thing in the morning so he can drive you and Max home as soon as Max is released."

Lucy was weary and worn out by then but more herself. "You don't have to do that. You can have Frank pick you up here and I can just drive my own car in the morning."

Rand shook his head firmly. "No. I don't want you driving. And if you need anything when you get home—prescriptions filled, groceries, anything—send Frank."

She didn't have the energy to argue so she just said, "Thank you. And thank you for everything today. I'm not sure I could have gotten through this without you."

"Don't thank me. It felt good to be needed. To take care of you. If you'd let me, I'd devote my life to doing just that."

It was the first reference he'd made to what had been going on between them when the phone call about Max had interrupted them. Lucy had almost forgotten about their fight, about the fact that she'd been in the middle of ending things with him.

But now she remembered it all. Sadly. But with no

less resignation. "It would make for a pretty boring life compared to what you're used to," she reiterated.

"I think it would be a pretty great life."

Lucy shook her head. "I meant what I said before," she whispered solemnly.

"Rethink it, Lucy," he commanded. "We make a good team."

"I do all right on my own," she said stubbornly, even as she knew she wouldn't have gotten through the day's ordeal without Rand. But she especially wouldn't admit that. It was too dangerous to acknowledge that she might need him or anyone else when the last time she'd felt that need she'd been left high and dry by a man so similar to Rand.

"Wouldn't do any harm to just give some consideration to letting me into your life permanently," Rand said.

But again she shook her head. "I don't have to think about it. I know what I'm doing and Max and I are better off alone."

Inside the hospital room Max stirred and Lucy rushed to his bedside while Rand looked in after her.

But Max hadn't actually awakened and after a turn of his head on the pillow he settled back into deep sleep.

Lucy didn't leave her son's bedside to return to Rand, though. She merely looked his way and said, "Thank you for everything," just as she might have said it to any stranger.

Rand seemed to get the message and left.

After all the time and distance from the emotions

of the morning, after all the other things that had replaced them during the day, Lucy didn't understand why she felt tears well up in her eyes as she watched him go.

Tears that had nothing to do with Max and everything to do with the feeling that her own heart was breaking in a way no amount of medicine could mend.

Ten

Monday dawned bright and sunny in California and the woman known as Meredith Colton was pleased to have an early morning phone call from the third private investigator she'd hired to locate her sister. She was also pleased to find herself alone in the house for a change so that there was no worry of being overheard.

"Well, what did you find?" she said eagerly into the receiver once the amenities were passed.

"I'm in Monterey. I spent the whole weekend buttering the palm of one of the nurses at the St. James Clinic here and following every lead I could find," the detective began.

"And?"

"I'm afraid the trail goes cold after the clinic."

"I hired you to tell me something I *don't* know."

"I can only tell you what I found out and it isn't much," he said. "Patsy Portman—who appeared from out of nowhere on the grounds of the clinic in 1992, disheveled, disoriented and mumbling about a car accident—was released after six months. At the time of her release she was still suffering from amnesia. She was, however, having frequent and vivid dreams and fragments of memories that led her doctors to be encouraged that the amnesia might resolve itself before too long. But due to the fact that she'd made a dramatic recovery from her years of anxiety, depression, mood swings, psychotic episodes and anti-social tendencies it was judged to her benefit to leave the clinic and pursue treatment of her amnesia as an outpatient. The trouble is, after her release she never returned to the clinic and there was no current address available," the investigator concluded.

"That's it?" the woman shouted.

"I told you the trail is cold after that. I can keep looking if you want but frankly I think it's a waste of your money. This isn't an uncommon occurrence. A lot of mentally ill or unbalanced people who improve in the hospital environment see a resurgence of their problems once they're out in the real world. If they don't return for care, some even end up as one of the homeless. That would account for the fact that there's no record of Patsy Portman from the time she left the clinic on. Those kind of people don't fare well on the streets. And even if they manage somehow, they don't last long. A high percentage of them end up dying as a Jane or John Doe and being buried in a pauper's grave. I can't guarantee it, but if I were betting on it, I'd say that's what we have here. Too many years have gone by without leaving a trace of her."

That calmed down the woman known as Meredith. In fact it was so comforting to her that she latched on to the explanation as if there were evidence to prove it.

"You're probably right," she agreed, taking a swift turnaround from her earlier outrage. "And if that's the case, there's no reason for you to look any further."

"Like I said, I can if you want me to, but I think it would be a waste of money. This Patsy Portman is long gone."

"No, you're right, there's no sense spending more money looking for a dead woman. Send me your bill and go ahead and call it quits."

And with that she hung up the phone, letting a smile play across her face as she allowed herself to believe she was out of the woods, that she no longer needed to worry about her sister cropping up to ruin things for her.

Which meant that now she could concentrate on the more pressing matter of that vile Emily....

Lucy didn't get Max home until noon on Monday. The recuperative powers of the child were amazing and by then he was bright and alert and, with the exception of the cast on his arm, showing almost no signs of the previous day's trauma.

Lucy, on the other hand, felt as if she'd been through the wringer. And it didn't help matters when she discovered on her coffee table a large wrapped package from Rand to Max.

Sadie came out from the kitchen at about the same time and said, "That arrived about an hour ago."

Once he'd determined it was for him, Max tore in to the wrapping and exclaimed delightedly over the treasure trove of dinosaur movies, picture books and coloring books and crayons.

"Did you see this?" he enthused to his mother and great-aunt. "Did you see what Rand got me? How come he did that?"

It was clear the present meant all the more to Max because it had come from his hero. A stab of pain went through Lucy to think that her son was already so attached to the man that he would miss him when Rand didn't come around anymore.

But she fought it and said as evenly as she could, "It's a get-well gift. When people are sick or have accidents and get hurt, other people send them presents."

"Cool!" the little boy said, his newest word since becoming friends with Mikey, the boy he'd been spending the night with when he'd decided to dive off the high bunk. "Can we call Rand and tell him to come over and play?"

The stabbing pain just got worse for Lucy. "No, we can't do that. I'm sure he's working."

"Then can we call him to come over tonight when he's not working?"

"I don't think we'll be seeing any more of Rand for a while, Max. But you can send him a thank-you picture, maybe one of the dinosaurs you color in the coloring books."

"But I want to see him myself and tell him thank you," the little boy insisted. "Why won't we see any more of him for a while? Is he going away on a trip or something?"

"Something," Lucy confirmed, distracting her son by pointing out that the plastic dinosaurs had come complete with their own rain forest for him to set up.

But Sadie was not so easily thrown off the track and once Max was occupied with his new toys she said, "Come into the kitchen with me, Lucy, and see if I made Max's Jell-O the way he likes it."

Since Max liked his Jell-O plain, Lucy knew it was a ploy but she had no choice, so she followed her aunt into the kitchen.

"What's going on?" Sadie asked without preamble.

"Right now I'd just like to take a shower and a nap," Lucy answered, pretending she didn't know what her aunt was referring to.

But Sadie would have none of that. "I don't mean what's going on here and now. I mean what's going on with you and Rand. Don't think I didn't notice at the hospital yesterday that Rand was dressed in the same clothes he picked you up in Saturday night—yes, I saw him, he was arriving just as I was leaving.

And you said yourself that the two of you rushed to
the hospital at six-thirty Sunday morning. It doesn't
take a genius to figure out he spent the night. Which,
by the way, I approve of since Max was out of the
house. But then last night in the corridor outside
Max's hospital room I could tell nothing good was
going on. Now you tell Max that Rand won't be coming around anymore. Something happened and I want
to know what it is.''

Sadie had always been the person Lucy confided
in, even as a child. It was only natural for her to do
that now despite some reluctance to rehash what she
would rather have been able to put behind her. So she
told her aunt the entire story, beginning to end, and
waited for Sadie to lend the unfailing support she had
in the past.

But that wasn't what Sadie did.

"You're wrong, Lucy," she said instead. "You're
so wrong."

"About what?" Lucy asked, surprised, defensive,
confused.

"About Rand. You're right that he lives a different
life than you do. You're right that he's put off having
a family because it would interfere with that life.
You're even right that he lives in a place that looks
more like a modern art museum than a house and that
Max would level it in a week. But Rand is a man who
knows himself. He's a man who says what he means
and means what he says. And if he says he's ready
to cut back on work, to have a family, ready to put
that family first, that's exactly what he's ready to do.''

"He'll regret it," Lucy contended, repeating part of the reasoning she'd already given her aunt.

"He doesn't make decisions he regrets. And he also doesn't bail out of things because he can't handle change. You may be talking about Rand but I think it's Marshall you have in mind."

"That's what Rand said. But they're very much alike."

"Maybe on the surface. But while Marshall liked a life that didn't accommodate having kids and wasn't willing to change, if Rand says he's willing to change to accommodate having a family, he is. Only you're not giving him the chance because you're projecting too much of your past onto the present. Onto him."

"He didn't even want a secretary with a child," Lucy reminded her aunt.

"And he probably still won't. But that doesn't mean he doesn't want to come home to a woman with a child. Or to that child." Sadie paused a moment as if to let that sink in and then said, "I know things have been hard for you since you got pregnant with Max, darling. I know you've made a lot of sacrifices for him. But I honestly don't think Rand is one of the things you have to give up for Max's sake. Or for any other reason. I think with Rand you can finally let down your guard and have what you want—and you do want him or I need my eyes checked. With Rand you can have what you deserve. What Max deserves. Trust me, Lucy. Trust Rand. You can, you know."

Trust Rand...

That was just what he'd asked her to do the night before. And she'd done it. Without regret.

But could she do it again, in the larger scheme of things?

Sadie left Lucy alone in the kitchen then, returning to Max with a bowl of the Jell-O she'd made him. Lucy didn't follow. Instead she crossed the kitchen to the window above the sink and looked out at the courtyard all four of her aunt's town houses shared.

But it wasn't the autumn-bare gardens or the tall cherry trees she saw out there. Her focus was all internal, all on what Sadie had said, all on thoughts of Rand.

It wasn't easy to shake the sense of how similar Rand and Marshall were on the surface. They were both well-respected, feared, high-powered movers and shakers in their own professions. They were both workaholics. They had both reached a point where concessions were made to them rather than them making concessions to anyone else.

Except that maybe that last part wasn't entirely true of Rand, she admitted to herself a little belatedly, feeling guilty for assigning something to him that might not be strictly true.

Yes, she'd done more adapting to him and his needs during the week she'd worked for him but he'd done some adjusting himself—working at her place, having Max to his, suspending work time while Max was with them so she could be with her son and see to his needs.

No, they hadn't been big alterations but they had

spoken of more flexibility than Marshall would have ever shown.

And maybe there was another difference between Marshall and Rand, too, she realized as she thought about it. Rand wasn't a selfish man, the way Marshall had been. Rand had been perfectly willing to share her with Max, which was something Marshall had told her point-blank he would never be willing to do. He'd said he had to be the center of the universe for whatever woman he was involved with and a child would only corrupt that. But Rand hadn't had any problems in that area. In fact he'd joined in when it came to Max. In some ways he'd taken over. It was part of why her son was so enamoured of him.

And Rand did know what being a part of a family entailed, she couldn't deny that. Not only had he come from a large one but he was so clear about the role a father needed to play in a family that he'd denied himself parenthood rather than come up short the way he'd felt his own father had at one time.

But on Sunday at the hospital he'd done just what a good father, a good husband, would have done, she had to admit. He'd suspended his own concerns to care for her and for Max. He couldn't have been more selfless, more compassionate, more caring, more helpful, even though they'd come from the discussion they'd had and the rejection she'd dished out.

So Rand had certainly proved that he could be there for her and Max when she needed him, which was definitely different from Marshall.

But could Rand make such a huge change in his lifestyle on a permanent basis?

She didn't know for sure.

But then, how could anyone know for sure?

Which was where the trust part of her aunt's lecture came in.

If she was going to allow Rand into her life, into Max's life, she would have to trust that he did know himself and what he wanted and what he was ready for.

And what he'd said he wanted was her. And Max.

That he'd said he was ready for was a family.

When she came down to that, a bubble of elation sprang to life inside her.

Rand wanted her...

Rand wanted Max...

Should she take the risk for them both?

She wanted to. More than she'd ever wanted anything.

She wanted Rand, and a family with him. She wanted Max to have him as his father.

If that had been what Rand had been proposing the morning before...

It occurred to Lucy that she wasn't exactly sure *what* Rand had been proposing. Suddenly that bubble of elation inside her lost some of its air.

What if he had only been proposing that they have some sort of other, uncommitted relationship?

That could put a whole new spin on things. A whole new spin that would put herself and Max more at risk than she was willing to.

But she'd never know unless she talked to Rand.

So talk to him.

She didn't want to do it over the phone and she couldn't leave Max right then, when she'd just gotten him home from the hospital.

"But there's still tonight," she whispered to herself.

Once she got Max to sleep, she could have Sadie baby-sit while she went to Rand's apartment.

Tension washed through her.

What if she'd misunderstood what he'd been leading up to the previous morning before she'd stopped him? What if she went there tonight and made a huge fool out of herself?

There was only one way to find out. So tonight she'd talk to him, she vowed.

If she could keep her courage up that long.

The doorman for Rand's apartment building recognized Lucy when she arrived at nine that evening but he wouldn't allow her to go up until first calling ahead.

That didn't help her nerves as she stood in the lobby waiting and imagining that Rand had another woman with him and had left orders with his doorman not to be disturbed.

Within moments she got the okay but the anxiety remained with her on the elevator. She hadn't only rejected Rand once yesterday, she'd rejected him twice. And now she couldn't help worrying that, even if he had intended something permanent, maybe after twenty-four hours of thinking about it, he'd gotten angry and would tell her to take a hike.

But she'd come this far and she wasn't going home without knowing exactly what he'd been suggesting the day before, even if her heart was in her throat and her knees felt as if they were made of jelly.

When the elevator doors opened on the eighth floor, Rand was standing in his open doorway, which cut short the idea of retreating back to the lobby, so she willed her legs to hold her up and stepped off the elevator.

"Is everything all right? Is Max okay?" Rand asked in greeting, clearly concerned that something bad had happened to bring her here.

"Everything is fine. Max is doing amazingly well," Lucy assured quietly, wanting to allay any worry as she crossed the outside hallway. She appreciated that he cared enough for that to be his first concern, though. It bolstered her decision to do what she was there to do.

From her pocket she took out a page torn from one of her son's new coloring books and handed it to Rand. Max had colored the picture and had her show him how to write thank you and his name at the top.

"Max wanted you to have this," she said. "He was about as excited as I've ever seen him to get home and find that gift from you. You've done enough. You didn't have to do that, too."

"I wanted to. But you didn't need to hand-deliver his thank-you. Especially not tonight."

Rand's expression was inscrutable and it didn't

make this any easier for her, particularly since he hadn't so much as invited her into his apartment. Again she worried that he might have female company. Female company who might have been helping him off with his clothes because he was down to just navy blue suit pants and an untucked, unbuttoned shirt that exposed a mind-numbingly sexy strip of chest and belly.

But again she summoned her courage to go headlong into her purpose for being there.

"I didn't just come to bring Max's picture. I wanted to talk to you," she finally admitted. "But if you aren't alone..."

"I'm alone," he said with an edge to his voice that let her know he was reading her thoughts and didn't appreciate the implication.

He stepped out of the doorway then, though, and made a sweeping gesture with his arm to indicate invitation.

Lucy went in, swallowing hard along the way and praying she was brave enough to go through with this as they stood facing each other in the entryway.

"Did you get a temp in today to work?" she asked, curious and trying to ease some of her own stress with small talk when he seemed inclined to have them remain in the foyer.

"The service sent over a pretty good one, actually. Sheila. She'll be back tomorrow and I may offer her the job."

"Young? Beautiful?" Lucy didn't know where that

had come from and she wished she could call the words back the moment they were out.

"She's about fifty, slightly plump, not attractive at all. But she's a great secretary."

"Good," Lucy said in a voice she barely recognized as her own.

Rand must have taken it to mean that she wasn't happy to have been replaced because he said, "I didn't think you'd be back. Between Max and—"

"No, it's good you found someone else. You're right, Max needs me at home."

Silence fell then as Lucy's courage flagged.

But after a moment Rand said, "Now tell me why you're really here."

There was no hostility in his tone. In fact there was a conservative sort of compassion that helped her to face him and say, "Sadie says I was wrong, and after thinking about it I've come to agree with her."

"What are you wrong about?"

"You." She took a deep breath and pushed herself to go on. "I'm sorry, Rand. It's just that Sunday morning when you started to talk about changing your life, I panicked. I had you all mixed up in my mind with Max's father and... Well, I was just wrong. I know that if you say you want to change your life you do. That you will. That you won't regret it. That you'll accomplish that as well as you've accomplished everything else."

"This sounds like an endorsement from an objective third party apologizing for not giving credit where credit is due. But is the punch line that you still don't want any part of it?''

''I don't know. That depends on what part of it you had in mind for me. I didn't let you get far enough to find out.''

''I was casting you as the leading lady.''

''What role exactly does the leading lady play? Steady girlfriend? Significant other?''

''You're still thinking of me as that other guy, Lucy. I'm talking about you being my wife.''

Relief washed over her and she smiled for the first time since her arrival. ''Oh.''

''That's all you have to say? Oh?''

''Is the offer still good?''

He took her hand in both of his and shook his head as if he couldn't believe she was asking that question. ''If you'll recall, I told you to think about it. So yes, the offer is still good. I'm in love with you, Lucy Lowry. I don't know how you could have missed it, but since you did—''

''A girl just likes to hear the words.''

''Okay. I love you. I love you. I love you. I love you so much that nothing is as important to me as being with you, as making you my wife, as making my life with you, as being a father to Max. I'd like it if you'd agree to marry me. And if you do, I promise you that I will never hurt you intentionally, and that I will always put you and Max and any other kids we might have first and foremost.''

''And you're sure?''

He rolled his eyes. "I'm sure. I'm positive. I'm absolutely certain. So what do you say?"

She didn't have to think about it. She said, "Yes. I say yes."

He stared down at her for a moment and she honestly thought he was going to pull her into his arms and kiss her. But instead he said, "I have one condition."

"You do?"

"I want you to let me be the breadwinner so you can go back to law school. You don't have to take a full load, just a few classes a semester while Max is in school. But I want you to go. I don't want to see that mind of yours wasted. And then, once you pass the bar, we can be partners in that, too."

Lucy laughed. If she'd had any lingering doubts about how different Rand was from Marshall, they disappeared in that instant because there wasn't a hint of the resentment for her ambitions that Marshall had always shown.

"I think you're just looking for a way to lighten your caseload," she joked.

"I'm looking for it all—wife, mother of my children, law partner, lover."

He finally did take her into his arms, kissing her a few playful, short kisses.

"Is Sadie with Max?" he asked between them.

"Yes."

"Is Max asleep?"

"Yes."

"So he wouldn't miss you if, say, it takes an hour or so for us to get back to him?"

"I don't think so," Lucy said, her voice growing deeper and more breathy as his kisses grew deeper and more passionate.

"Think Sadie would mind?"

"She figured out that you spent Saturday night with me and said she approved, so I don't think she'd mind."

Rand smiled. "That's my girl."

He kissed Lucy's neck then, just below her earlobe at a spot she'd never realized was so sensitive, so arousing.

"And what about you? Any qualms about sticking around here for a little while?"

"Depends on what for," she teased, tilting her head to allow more of the feather-brush of his lips against her skin.

"For this," he said in a husky voice as he slipped off the coat she was still wearing and reached beneath her sweater to massage her bare back while his mouth returned to hers in open, hungry kisses that wiped away all other thoughts.

Even though Lucy had believed she'd given herself over to Rand when they'd made love before, she learned then that she hadn't. Not the way she did now.

Now, when his hands grazed her flesh, shedding her clothes and his.

Now, when he led her to his bedroom and laid her on the downy comforter, lying beside her, capturing her mouth and claiming her breasts with his wondrous hands. Now, when her own hands claimed him in return.

Now, when she opened to him, accepted him fully into her and rode the wild ride with him that sealed the union they'd finally made, that celebrated it and bound them together for all of eternity.

And when they lay spent and exhausted and holding each other, Lucy finally said the words she'd thought she might never again say to anyone but Max. "I love you."

Rand chuckled slightly. "I was wondering if I was ever going to hear that from you."

"I like to keep you guessing. It stokes the fires."

"I don't think you'll have any problem stoking my fires. And by the way, in case you've forgotten, I love you, too."

She knew that. But it was still good to hear again. In fact, she couldn't imagine ever hearing it enough.

"I should get home," she told him on a reluctant sigh.

"*We* should get home," he amended and it sounded incredibly good to her.

Still she didn't hurry to move. She allowed herself just a little while to savor being there in Rand's arms, reveling in his love for her, in her love for him, in the fact that she'd found him just when she'd been certain there wasn't anyone out there she could trust again.

But there had been. There had been just one man who was perfect for her, who would be perfect for her for the rest of her life. Perfect for Max, too, whom she knew would be thrilled to welcome Rand into their small family.

And a family was just what they'd be, she thought.

A wonderful, loving family.

A family that really could have that happily-ever-after she'd thought was too good to be true.

*   *   *   *   *

Don't miss the next book in
the Colton series—PASSION'S LAW
by Ruth Langan
in November 2001.

One

"**D**etective." Heather brought a hand to her throat in a gesture of surprise. "I didn't hear you."

There was a breathy quality to her voice that intrigued him. If he hadn't noticed it earlier in her uncle's office, he'd write it off as nerves. Without realizing it, his frown deepened. He took a step closer, until they were mere inches apart.

With each step that he took toward her, she had an almost overpowering urge to step back, out of reach. Foolish, she knew, but the feeling was too strong to deny. This man made her uncomfortable. Odd, since she'd never before been anything but completely comfortable in the presence of men. But then, this man wasn't like any she'd ever met.

Though she thought of herself as tall, she had to

tip her head back to see his face. He had to be several
inches over six feet, with broad shoulders and a
powerfully muscled chest. For a big man he moved
with surprising catlike grace.

"Sorry. I didn't mean to startle you." His voice
was low and deep, with a hint of impatience.

"You could have warned me you were here." She
had the distinct impression that he'd been there for
some time, watching her, and had been as uncomfortable as she when she'd turned and caught sight of
him.

"And interrupt those deep thoughts of yours?"

So, he had been watching her.

When he drew close she saw again that piercing
stare. It had the strangest effect on her. She'd thought
his eyes dark, but in the sunlight streaming through
the windows she could see that they were a deep
midnight blue.

A breeze flitted through the open window, flinging
a lock of her hair across her face. Without warning
he lifted a finger to it and brushed it aside. It was the
slightest touch, and yet it sent a jolt of electricity
charging through her system with all the force of a
lightning bolt.

At that simple touch she stood perfectly still,
absorbing the tremors that rocked her. Her eyes
widened and she had to clasp her hands together to
keep from flinching.

Had he felt it too, or was she the only one affected
like this? A quick glance at his face revealed only a
slight narrowing of his eyes. But it was enough to tell

her that he wasn't as cool and disinterested as he tried to appear.

He cleared his throat. "Did I understand that you're going to be living here?"

She nodded, afraid to trust her voice.

"For how long?"

She swallowed and prayed she wouldn't sound as uneasy as she felt. "I don't really know." She looked at him, then away. "I guess I'll be here for as long as my uncle needs me."

"Needs you for what?"

"He's been spending most of his time here since the…" She couldn't bring herself to mention the shooting. "Since his party. And because I'm familiar with the work, I offered to come here and act as his assistant."

"I see." He glanced around. "Have you considered the isolation of this place?"

She nodded. "That's part of its charm."

"For a week or two maybe. After that, when people realize they can't shop at high-priced boutiques, or reserve a table at a fancy restaurant, the charm starts to wear thin. How long do you think you can stand it, Miss McGrath?"

"I told you. For as long as my uncle needs me."

"Even if it turns out to be months?"

She nodded. "That's right." She arched a brow. "Is that a look of skepticism, Detective?"

"Could be. Personally I doubt you'll last more than a week or two before you get the urge to race back to civilization."

"Is that so? You wouldn't care to bet on that, would you?"

For the first time his lips curved slightly, the only hint of humor. "Are you asking a man of the law to gamble?"

"Afraid you'll lose?"

He continued staring at her. "Are you a betting woman, Miss McGrath?"

"I've been known to make a wager or two."

"Have you now?" He gave her a measuring look that had the heat rising to her cheeks. "Five bucks says you're bored out of your mind and out of here within two weeks." He stuck out his hand. "Deal?"

She glanced down at his hand, then up into those challenging eyes. "Oh, yeah. How can I resist such an easy way to make five dollars? You're on, Detective."

He closed his hand over hers and, too late, she remembered how she'd felt the first time his hand had held hers. The heat was back, racing along her spine, surging through her veins. But when she tried to break free, he merely drew her closer, until his lips hovered just above hers. "My friends call me Thad."

"Really?" She wanted to look away, but wouldn't give him the satisfaction. Instead she lifted her head, forcing herself to meet that steely gaze. "Then I guess I'll call you Detective Law, because I don't see the two of us becoming friends. Would you like to pay up now? Or are you going to make me wait until the two weeks are up?"

He chuckled. He'd give her this much. She didn't

back down. "You haven't won anything yet, Miss McGrath. As for me, I think my job just got more interesting."

"Your job?" She was suddenly alert as she yanked her hand free and studied him more carefully. "You're...working here? I thought this was just a routine visit and that you wouldn't be back."

"Sorry to disappoint you."

For the first time she noticed the notepad in his other hand. Her voice lowered. "If this isn't merely a routine check, does this mean something is wrong?"

He kept his features deliberately unreadable. "Sorry, Miss McGrath. I'm not at liberty to discuss my business with anyone except your uncle."

"Of course." She felt the sting of censure and wondered how it was that this man could make her feel so damnably awkward. In any other man his attitude would come across as pure arrogance, but she had the feeling that in Thad Law, it was simply the way he conducted business. No doubt he put up a wall between himself and every civilian he came in contact with.

"Well." She took a step back, needing to put some distance between them so she could catch her breath. "Don't let me stop you, Detective."

Instead of giving her the space she so obviously wanted, he leaned close and watched the way her eyes narrowed. "I told you. It's Thad. Why don't you try it?"

"Why don't you—" She drew in a breath when

she saw the hint of humor in his eyes. She counted to ten, then tried again. "Okay. Why not? I guess I'll be seeing you around, Thad."

"You can count on it, Miss McGrath."

"My name is Heather."

He seemed to consider that a moment, as though fitting the name to the woman. "You can count on seeing me around, Heather." He stood there a moment longer, feeling the tension hum between them. Then he turned on his heel.

She watched him walk away. It occurred to her that he didn't so much walk as stalk. Like a panther on the trail of some poor, unsuspecting prey.

She shivered at the thought.

Crossing her arms over her chest, she waited until her breathing had returned to normal and her legs felt steady enough to carry her without stumbling. Then she headed in the opposite direction. She didn't want to bump in to Thaddeus Law again. There was something far too dark and dangerous about him.

THE COLTONS

Silhouette®
Where love comes alive™

If you've enjoyed getting to know **THE COLTONS**,
Silhouette® invites you to come back and
visit the Colton family!

Just collect three (3) proofs of
purchase from the backs of three (3) different
COLTONS titles and receive a free **COLTONS**
book that's not currently available in retail outlets!

Just complete the order form and send it, along with three
(3) proofs of purchase from three (3) different **COLTONS**
titles, to: **THE COLTONS**, P.O. Box 9047, Buffalo, NY
14269-9047, or P.O. Box 613, Fort Erie, Ontario L2A 5X3.

(No cost for shipping and handling.)

Name: _____

Address: _____ City: _____

State/Prov.: _____ Zip/Postal Code: _____

Please specify which title(s) you would like to receive:

❑ 0-373-38716-4 *PROTECTING PEGGY* by Maggie Price
❑ 0-373-38717-2 *SWEET CHILD OF MINE* by Jean Brashear
❑ 0-373-38718-0 *CLOSE PROXIMITY* by Donna Clayton
❑ 0-373-38719-9 *A HASTY WEDDING* by Cara Colter

Remember—for each title selected, you must send three (3)
original proofs of purchase. To receive *all four (4)* titles, just send
in all twelve (12) proofs of purcha

(Please allow 4-6 weeks for delivery.
Offer good while quantities last.
Offer available in Canada and the U.S. only.)
(The proof of purchase should be cut off the

093 KIJ DAET   Visit Silhouette at www

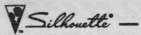

If you enjoyed what you just read,
then we've got an offer you can't resist!

Take 2
bestselling novels FREE!
Plus get a FREE surprise gift!

Clip this page and mail it to The Best of the Best™

IN U.S.A.
3010 Walden Ave.
P.O. Box 1867
Buffalo, N.Y. 14240-1867

IN CANADA
P.O. Box 609
Fort Erie, Ontario
L2A 5X3

YES! Please send me 2 free Best of the Best™ novels and my free surprise gift. After receiving them, if I don't wish to receive anymore, I can return the shipping statement marked cancel. If I don't cancel, I will receive 4 brand-new novels every month, before they're available in stores! In the U.S.A., bill me at the bargain price of $4.24 plus 25¢ shipping and handling per book and applicable sales tax, if any*. In Canada, bill me at the bargain price of $4.74 plus 25¢ shipping and handling per book and applicable taxes**. That's the complete price and a savings of over 15% off the cover prices—what a great deal! I understand that accepting the 2 free books and gift places me under no obligation ever to buy any books. I can always return a shipment and cancel at any time. Even if I never buy another book from The Best of the Best™, the 2 free books and gift are mine to keep forever.

185 MEN DFNG
385 MEN DFNH

Name	(PLEASE PRINT)	
Address	Apt.#	
City	State/Prov.	Zip/Postal Code

* Terms and prices subject to change without notice. Sales tax applicable in N.Y.
** Canadian residents will be charged applicable provincial taxes and GST.
   All orders subject to approval. Offer limited to one per household and not valid to
   current Best of the Best™ subscribers.
   ® are registered trademarks of Harlequin Enterprises Limited.

BOB01   ©1998 Harlequin Enterprises Limited

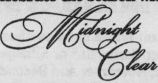

Celebrate the season with

Midnight Clear

A holiday anthology featuring
a classic Christmas story from
New York Times bestselling author

Debbie Macomber

Plus a brand-new *Morgan's Mercenaries* story
from *USA Today* bestselling author

Lindsay McKenna

And a brand-new *Twins on the Doorstep* story
from national bestselling author

Stella Bagwell

Available at your favorite retail outlets in November 2001!

Silhouette®

Where love comes alive™

CALL THE ONES YOU LOVE OVER THE HOLIDAYS!

Save $25 off future book purchases when you buy any four Harlequin® or Silhouette® books in October, November and December 2001,

PLUS

receive a phone card good for 15 minutes of long-distance calls to anyone you want in North America!

WHAT AN INCREDIBLE DEAL!

Just fill out this form and attach 4 proofs of purchase (cash register receipts) from October, November and December 2001 books, and Harlequin Books will send you a coupon booklet worth a total savings of $25 off future purchases of Harlequin® and Silhouette® books, AND a 15-minute phone card to call the ones you love, anywhere in North America.

Please send this form, along with your cash register receipts
as proofs of purchase, to:
In the USA: Harlequin Books, P.O. Box 9057, Buffalo, NY 14269-9057
In Canada: Harlequin Books, P.O. Box 622, Fort Erie, Ontario L2A 5X3
Cash register receipts must be dated no later than December 31, 2001.
Limit of 1 coupon booklet and phone card per household.
Please allow 4-6 weeks for delivery.

I accept your offer! Enclosed are 4 proofs of purchase. Please send me my coupon booklet and a 15-minute phone card:

Name: _____

Address: _____ City: _____

State/Prov.: _____ Zip/Postal Code: _____

Account Number (if available): _____

---

097 KJB DAGL
PHQ4013

THE COLTONS

If you missed the first four exciting stories
from **THE COLTONS**, here's a chance
to order your copies today!

0-373-38704-0	BELOVED WOLF by Kasey Michaels	$4.50 U.S.☐ $5.25 CAN.☐
0-373-38705-9	THE VIRGIN MISTRESS by Linda Turner	$4.50 U.S.☐ $5.25 CAN.☐
0-373-38706-7	I MARRIED A SHEIK by Sharon De Vita	$4.50 U.S.☐ $5.25 CAN.☐
0-373-38707-5	THE DOCTOR DELIVERS	
	by Judy Christenberry	$4.50 U.S.☐ $5.25 CAN.☐

(limited quantities available)

TOTAL AMOUNT	$ _____
POSTAGE & HANDLING	$ _____
($1.00 for one book, 50¢ for each additional)	
APPLICABLE TAXES*	$ _____
TOTAL PAYABLE	$ _____

(check or money order—please do not send cash)

To order, send the completed form, along with a check or money order for the
total above, payable to **THE COLTONS**, to: In the U.S.: 3010 Walden Avenue,
P.O. Box 9077, Buffalo, NY 14269-9077; In Canada: P.O. Box 636, Fort Erie,
Ontario L2A 5X3.

Name: _____

Address: _____ City: _____

State/Prov.: _____ Zip/Postal Code: _____

Account # (if applicable): _____ 075 CSAS

*New York residents remit applicable sales taxes.
Canadian residents remit applicable GST and provincial taxes.

Visit Silhouette at www.eHarlequin.com
COLTBACK-4